Nine Island

Also by Jane Alison

The Love-Artist
The Marriage of the Sea
Natives and Exotics
The Sisters Antipodes

As Translator

Change Me: Stories of Sexual Transformation from Ovid

Nine Island

Jane Alison

Catapult
New York

Published by Catapult
catapult.co

ISBN: 978-1-936787-12-8

Catapult titles are distributed to the trade by
Publishers Group West, a division of the Perseus Book Group
Phone: 800-788-3123

Library of Congress Control Number: 2015955988

Printed in the United States of America

9 8 7 6 5 4 3 2 1

For ARK
and in memory of G

ONE

So I'VE SAILED the seas and come to—

No. I've sailed no seas. I've driven south down I-95, driven south for days, until 95 stopped and I was back in Miami.

No country for old women.

I'm not old yet, but my heart is sick with old desire, and I'm back in this place of sensual music to see if it's time to retire from love.

What a delight to be free of that maddening monster, lust!

So Plato claims Sophocles said.

Could be.

I'd just spent a month with *you*, Sir Gold, up where 95 starts. After thirty years since I'd seen you last, thirty years of disaster with men, one day you dropped from the sky to my in-box. Your name there I looked at a very long time.

Ahoy! you finally said when I clicked.

First we had a yearlong exchange of pictures and words. Then I flew up for a week of ceviche, strolls through hydrangeas, Greek pots. Then you asked me to come again and stay awhile in your stone house on a hill.

These words I looked at a long time, too.

Bring Ovid! you said. Bring the cat.

Are you here yet? you said, when I'd just started driving.

You smoked me a trout, yanked armfuls of greens out of your ground, made me a tarte tatin. You even filled your swimming pool just so I could swim!

Gazing down at the naked older me, you murmured, Look at that.

Later you said, Isn't this funny, after so many years.

Come *closer*, you murmured in the dark.

And in the morning: happy whistling as you strode over wet grass with the dog, then bounded back to me still in bed.

I thought, Could it *be*?

Happy end?

But when the month was done—well, who knows. Your hazel-green eyes went pained, and you decided it best to stay as you were, just the dog, the stone house, the hill.

Thanks for coming up, though!

I ramped onto 95 south thinking, *Really* ought to give up on all this.

Sobs shook the Mini, rock songs blasting to heighten the pain, for seven high-speed hours.

But give up on *what*, exactly, I have to ask myself.

Has it not been decades of comical disaster?

Should be good to give up on disaster.

I stopped near Annapolis to see my mother. *She* is a lady who's sailed the seas of love, all the way from Australia. She's had a long career in men, trailing me along through husbands, then boyfriends, then the species of men who vanish by daybreak, until finally the seas dried up and she landed alone. She knows all about my wandering. Erring, as she calls it.

You, too? she said to me once. Oh, my darling dear.

When I parked outside her house in Woods Landing, she came to the door and wavered, silky as ash: she wobbles and lists even sitting. Loss of labyrinthine function, doctors say, a phrase that has bewitched us. She insists it isn't dizziness; the horizon just started tilting one day, and she can't get it to stop.

I came in and watched her lurch and careen from wall to fridge, then tumble into a chair, surrounded by her carved and painted birds, clutching the table for safety.

Look at you! I said to her. This has to end. You need a plan. Do you hear me? A plan for where to live next. It's *time*.

She tossed her head and glanced away. Let's not talk about *me*, she said. Let's talk about you, bossy girl. How'd it go?

Meaning the month. She'd heard about Sir Gold three decades ago, when he first broke my heart. Then much, much more about him this year, when it all seemed so hopeful again.

I shook my head.

She pondered me. After a moment, sighed.

Well, she said, placing her spotted hand on mine. Well, well. Maybe, darling, you should give up on all that. Maybe it's just *time*.

Got back in the car and drove blurrily south.

Last chance lost! Odyssey done!

From Annapolis down around D.C., through Virginia, North Carolina, South. Trees changed from oaks to loblollies to palmettos among pines as the sun freckled my hands, mottled my chest. Buster was with me, have I said that? Buster, my darling, the only real one. Skinny and black with a white spot on his nose, almost entirely blind and deaf, paws flailing for knowledge.

Three decades of wandering among men. I *have* to ask myself, For what? Who made them the trees, the stars?

Boys at seven running after you and knocking you down, sticky lips all over your face. Boys in alleys, on sand dunes, in cars; boys on tables, on stairs, in closets. Skinny blond painter with fish eyes I lived with awhile, tall architect with an eclipse in one eye and long hands that shook. The one I married and stayed with for years . . . Then the wretched end of that and it was back to the start: a heat-seeking tour of old boyfriends. Who knew? Might be something I'd missed. Wrote to old boyfriends from decades before—college, high school, one from fifth grade—the kind that really *know* you and send messages back that fill you with hope. *Have thought about you often! Would love to see you. Come!* The tour took me up and down I-95, involved lots of nervous drinking and ruinous sex, but one old boyfriend after another in flesh was not what he'd been in ether, and not at *all* what he'd been before. First was Lurch, then Mick, Sad Eyes, the Devil. But they turned out even more errant than me: girlfriends or wives kept secret in pockets, vessels broken on once noble noses, gazing into glasses of gin.

And this was when Sir Gold appeared, drifting back into my life like a cloud.

Nel mezzo del cammin di nostra vita . . .

Just halfway along the footpath of life
I looked up, alarmed—I was in a dark wood . . .

Pine forests, pine barrens. Swamps.

In Georgia I stopped at a hotel with walls made of oyster shells jammed in concrete, and in its saloon I ate shrimp and grits and drank too much wine for a woman alone, helplessly checking for messages. Someone—*you*—saying, Come back!

Such a sickness, wanting. No end?

After the hotel of shells came the zone of orange groves. I'm skipping the miles of spattered asphalt, turtles pondering on the side of the road, gas stations, Waffle Houses, outlets for cigarettes or perfume, trucks with no qualms about blasting my Mini to the shoulder. But we recover fast and mad, no trouble getting in their way again and making them lose time. Once we were in Florida, I gazed into the orange groves. Groves to the east, groves to the west, slanting corridors of citrus, the sun biblical as it set beyond them, an almighty crown of light.

Then 95 ended and I was back in Miami. Where I'd moved two years ago, fresh from marriage and shaky, true, but full of hope and vim. Such vim! LIVE IN PARADISE, the ad had said. I'd looked up at all the glass shining high in the sky, enormous white clouds pulsing. Energy in that upper air: ions spun through deepening blue, singing LIVE THE LIFE!

But below that sky of dancing ions, up and down Route 1: billboards for breast augmentation.

A clue.

DROVE EAST OVER the Venetian Causeway toward my island, Belle Isle, with Buster, Ovid, Latin dictionaries, notes, an invisible trail of exhaust. Biscayne Bay glinted green all around.

Haven't really mentioned Ovid yet.

He's been my guide through the land o' love from the start.

Take my hand, he whispered when I was eighteen. *I'll walk you through the thickets of love and sing you strange stories to help you see.*

In fact I first met *you*, Sir Gold, the day I first read Ovid. A Tuesday: Latin in the morning, Painting at night.

I was sitting cross-legged on the studio floor when a voice like a breeze in branches murmured, Got an extra pencil?

I looked up: a golden boy's face, hazel-green eyes as startled as mine, looking down at me.

Pure light.

It happens, you know. Shaft in the heart.

It took us both a moment to stir, but he's the one who moved first. He shook his head slightly and turned.

Me: I was done. Soon I followed him helplessly from party to party, followed that torn suede jacket slung from his shoulders as he strode and laughed away. And when he happened to cross my path and those eyes caught mine—all words flew from my head.

Late at night: I'd hover mute and drunk outside his door, too miserable to knock.

Help me, help me, help me with this pain! I'd wail into the night, stumbling home on the flagstones.

Ovid whispered, *Echo and Narcissus.*

And turned the pain to art.

Echo, who wanted a beautiful boy but had nothing to give, could not even speak for herself. Who'd want her? She pined and pined, wasted away, finally turned into rocks. Stones, bones. A voice hanging around in the air.

Motored over the Venetian Causeway from the tollbooth to San Marino Island, past more glinting bay, and on to Di Lido Island and Rivo Alto, passing palazzi, modern white boxes, extravaganzas of blossoms and fronds.

Orange sign on the shoulder:

DRAWBRIDGE AHEAD.

Which made me think:

DRAW BRIDGE A HEAD.

Which made me think:

TWO MEN WALKING ABREAST.

Which made me think:

Of him. *Again*. A joke he once made when by magic I sat with him somewhere, trying not to melt in his eyes.

TWO MEN WALKING A BREAST.

He drew it and slid the picture my way. Two men and between them, a breast on a leash.

See? he said, see? And laughed with himself, looked hurt that I didn't, tucked the picture away.

But the girl he finally married instead of me when I was too much trouble: that's the kind of cancer that took her.

The bell clanged cars to a stop at the drawbridge, so I got out to watch the bridge slowly split. Walked to the edge of the grassy verge and looked over the water to my island. Belle Isle, once called Bull Isle for the bulls that used to graze there, before a new, more belle clientele moved in. On it my building loomed huge and gray.

The yacht nosed between the piers and glided near, long and sleek and shark-gilled. On its snout lay a black-haired girl in a moon-white bikini. As she drifted past, she tilted her head to the setting sun, and her eyes fell upon me. We gazed at each other through filmy air, her flesh emitting light.

F OR INSTANCE (here comes one of those stories by Ovid):

He sings of a girl on a beach who's coaxed by a bull to climb onto his back. For "bull" be imaginative, please: let it be a metaphor. Understand these poems of Ovid's as code. So. The bull's lowered himself, bone-white elbows in the sand, making a place for her toes. As soon as she's up, knobby knees digging into his flanks, he rises and plunges with her into the sea. Wild waves! What can she do? She holds on tight, fingers wrapped around his horns. Surely it's more dangerous to let go and fall in than let herself be taken? Look how dark that water is!

"Take" in Latin = *rapere*: rape.

"Taken" in Australia = eaten by a shark.

I might have the girl ride a shark instead, when I transmute Ovid's stories.

Just grab the fin, said a stepfather once as he lounged on the sand with *The Washington Post* and a beer. His long dark legs were crossed at the ankle, smoke rising from his hand.

If you're swimming way the hell out there, he said, and you see a big fin coming your way? Just grab it.

Then what?

Ride!

But what if I let go?

Well. He shrugged, laughed, flicked his cigarette away. I guess then he'll *get* you.

Sometimes you make a bad choice in these matters, of men and horns and fins.

Sometimes it seems no choice is good.
And really, I lie when I ask who made men the trees, the stars.
Almighty fathers and stepfathers: that's who.

OUT ON MY balcony on the twenty-first floor, a wineglass sweats between my legs, my fingertips filming the keyboard. Miami Beach glitters and roars over the bay; beyond it, vast black sea.

SPECTACULAR BAY VIEWS!! POOL GYM MARINA TENNIS KOI PONDS SO MUCH MORE!!! LIVE THE LIFE!!!!

Well, the ad was true enough. There's the bay, full of boats and lights and glossy black. Twenty stories down is the gym; around back, the pool, koi ponds, marina.

Am sipping and pondering this life to be lived, while inside Buster navigates the floor. He's grown more blind in the month we were gone. He leans a skinny black shoulder against a wall and creeps forward until a chair or table stops him, then wavers with opaque eyes until deciding to push onward. His little black body creeps over the cork floor, beneath maps of water cities and islands, beneath shelves of books about color and plants, beneath my desk stacked high with Ovid.

Boats glint down in the bay, their lights and the lights' liquid ghosts.

Across the way, at Costa Brava, the next big condo on Island Avenue, a man has just stepped out to a balcony—and he appears to be naked.

Can't quite see—balcony rail is in the way. But I think I see the tender flesh channel at the hip.

The one it can be so nice to run a tongue along, at times. On one's way to delectable firmness.

Swallow a mouthful of wine and ponder. Is it really time to retire from love?

Ovid does not like women who drink too much.

Trying not to do that.

But tell me. Should I stay? Or should I go?

My friend K from South Carolina, with fiery blond hair and furious thumbs and the fastest mouth I've ever heard, types me her opinion:

You are NOT ready to retire, dammit. Put on that bikini, I don't care how old you are, and go out and live that life.

THE MORNING AIR of paradise rolls in molten waves over your skin when you slide open the balcony door and dip out a hand, glass and tiles so hot they hurt. Inside, Buster has puddled the floor—hard to see puddles on the swirling patterns of cork, and I skidded in two before coffee. Wiped them up with yellow gloves, wondering what to do next.

Ignore problem and put on bikini, that's what. Not a minute to spare to go out and start living the et cetera.

Out my door I went in old polka-dot bikini, carrying towel and books.

This *building* is old, not old old but Miami old, circa 1980. I knew it when I rented the place two years ago but see it harshly now. The building's public areas, as they're called, are full of heavy woodwork, mirrors, brass sconces fixed crooked to the walls, and along the curving hallways whose floors aren't level—is that true? building sinking into sand, or what?—lies worn carpet with dull vegetal patterns that maybe once were green and orange but now are beige and dun. Door after door, brass sconce after crooked brass sconce, three of them flickering out. A smell. In the elevator are mirrors with cut-glass flamingos and, as the doors slid open today, a little pink man named Lino. In a white linen suit, strands of white hair beneath a white hat. He looked like a lascivious elderly elf.

Hello! he said as I stepped in. Do you live here?

I certainly do, I said, as I say each time he asks.

He eyed me. You don't look like you do.

Yet I do. For now!

Ha, he said. We're all just here for now. But anyway. If you live here, you better make sure your husband's a lawyer. Is your husband a lawyer?

Said no. Asked why.

Because the board's a bunch of crooks, he said. All those guys, they're going to ruin us. The pool, he said. They say it needs to be demolished. The whole thing replaced. The pool and koi ponds and garden and parking garage beneath it, the whole shebang. And you know why? Because they're all in the concrete business. They're crooks. Boy, do they stand to make out big—on us! Special assessments up the wazoo! So you better make sure your husband's a lawyer.

I'll try, I said. Okay, this is me.

The doors opened, he tipped his hat, I stepped out.

Was this true? Good god. No way could I afford it—my landlord would for sure pass it straight on to me.

On the mezzanine (a.k.a. second floor) is the restaurant offering early-bird specials; also the gym, where the bikes and running machines all rest; plus the card room, empty. No one up or down the long hall, just mirrors showing me, alarmed.

Have been here two years and only now see: it's a cruise ship. Empty old Love Boat. Once all the pairs have walked the plank and gone on.

Wait, still here! Wait!

But out back is the paradise jungle, ah, deep cool tropical shade. A pink concrete path winds past koi streams, through a jungle of fans and spines and huge shapely leaves, and at the end of the greenery: a blue pool like an hourglass. Still and clear, not a ripple, no stir, an hourglass full of sky.

There was once a limpid pool, whispered Ovid—and I broke into a panicked run.

Towel and books dumped on a lounge chair, dress shrugged off: crash in.

Cool blue water pleats at your hands as you glide!

Floating in the hourglass pool . . .

Its slender waist, voluptuous volumes of blue.

Touch a woman where she most likes, says Ovid, *touch her just right in her tiny pond, and you will see her eyes glow.*

Opened legs to the water and winged out my arms, shutting eyes so only they knew if they glowed.

Twenty laps later, I clung gasping to the concrete lip, the building's nine o'clock shadow cloaking the pool. Twenty-four floors (I counted, I count things, even when I already know), twenty-four stories times seven balconies (it's good to do math when you can, keeps the brain sharp), all those balconies and potential eyes looking over this pool, jungle, and bay to Miami. But no one on any of them, no one in any of the lounge chairs surrounding the pool.

Alone, alone, all, all alone, alone on a wide wide—

No. Jorge was hosing philodendra in his rubber boots and white hat. I slung a wet wave his way; he waved back. A green heron on a branch above the koi pond stared into the water.

I climbed out, wrapped torso in towel, walked along the cracked pink path through the paradise jungle, past the hot tubs nestled in shiny dark green. One still bubbled a chlorine bloom, and on the path—a trail of wet feet. Followed. But they grew fainter and smaller in the sun and were gone by the spiraling concrete steps to the dock. Spiraled down myself, past the silver-pink tree that is in fact a girl who ran from something and had to shoot headfirst into the ground to escape. Her slender trunk rises from the soil to a belly, then splits into two slim legs; between them, a delicate girl-cleft.

So lifelike: I admire her each time I pass.

No one on the wide, curving dock, just a bucket and another trail of wet on the planks at berth number five. The dock has berths for thirty-six boats—I don't have to count, they're numbered. *Tango* and *All In!* and others just like them, all sleek-shark yachts except my favorite, *Paradise Found*. That is its name, in happy white cursive. A miniature ferry, red with chrome trim. From the dock you could step over the water to its little back porch and open a door to a cabin with sliding windows, white-cushioned couches along the sides, a wet bar, you can see it—a place just like a honeymoon. Imagine living there, bobbing on the sea. Good morning! Sailor cap on head, blouse knotted at waist, stepping out into warm blue from happy warm sheets. Ahoy! And at night, at night, the stars aglow, music veiling the glittering dark.

A place for Marilyn Monroe. Yes. I can see her slinking around in there, creamy and gold, with a glass of champagne and those big eyes, shy.

Oh, Marilyn. Who couldn't have babies and didn't want to grow old.

Deep below the boats, through the transparent green, lie sunken concrete chunks, barnacled and slick with kelp. Also a labyrinthine-brain coral I check on often to make sure it's alive. Long needle-nose fish hang in the water, sometimes Portuguese men-of-war with their blue balloons and wicked tendrils, or moon jellies, tarpon; sometimes a manatee rolls up and snorts.

Always worth peering into the water. Almost living the life.

A large darkness down there suddenly stirred—I froze. From it moved a slender black length that became a fin, and then a black-gloved hand. A head appeared, slowly turned, and Heathcliff eyes stared up at me through a mask before slipping below the hull.

Hurried to the other side of the boat and peered into the depths: nothing. Down there slithering invisibly around?

Heathcliff! It's me! I've come home!

Went to the end of the dock and squinted up at my building, so tall it seemed to tumble from the blue and the clouds. On a high balcony appeared someone—that incredibly thin woman with white-blond hair, could see how skinny she was from all those stories below. She looked out at the bay, then straight down to the ground. She stepped from view, came back to the rail. Then reached out her arm, paused, and let something drop.

She leaned out to watch it fall.

I looked at where it must have landed, then back up the building to her. But she was resting her elbows on the rail now, neck stretched long, gazing far.

ACTUALLY, THAT white-blond woman is a key. Part of the code re the economics of love. That skinny woman and her man: I've looked at them a lot this past year. Out by the pool, he reads the paper, he never looks up, he rests ankle on knee and reads. His hand reaches for a drink, but his eyes don't leave the page. His flesh is smooth and tanned and full, *pinguis* in Latin, health glowing through his skin; as the sun rolls over, his shoulders shine, his golden-gray hair gleams. Supreme self-possession is what I see. Beside him, she agitates. In her skinny skin, those thin, thin bones, those large liquid eyes running in her drawn face. She lies down, sits up, looks around, twists, stands, paces with big hands locked behind her back, looks over the bay, turns to stare at the building, the pool, the man she married, who all the while sits absorbed in his paper. She's half his size: tanned bones.

A woman who wants, a man who wants nothing. These two have stalked the world for thousands of years. Penia and Poros. Echo, Narcissus.

Another female like that is an Ovid monster named Hunger. One hundred percent ravenousness, Hunger whistles and whirls into your room at night, crouches on your chest, glues her nasty mouth to yours, and breathes her neediness into you. From then on you are full of want.

Wanting is exactly what I've never wanted.

I drew Echo once as a skeletal girl like Hunger, bone hand reaching, face all mouth, to explain what I feared most.

The golden boy considered the drawing, looked pained, then slid it back over the table.

Some things, he said, should probably stay private.

ONE VERSION OF the birth of erotic love:

Penia (female, = Want) raped Poros (male, = Want Nothing), because she wanted what he *was*.

The child Penia bore, the child of Want and Want Nothing?

Eros, a.k.a. Love.

You can spend some time pondering the logic and logistics of this.

So:

Should I stay?

Or should I go?

Just what is meant by "I," anyway?

Look at it! Skinny little skeletal stalk, so simple and neat, coming not even close to conveying the runny, yolky mess it stands for.

"Ego" is better if you want to say "I." Even *ich*. Or *io* or *je* or *yo*.

Let's be decisive and say, Go.

Yes.

It will be tonic, throwing away want all at once. Closing the door and saying, I'm done.

Sono chiuso, as an Italian lady once said, pushing away her plate. I'm shut.

What a relief!

Seal the leaky jar.

And remember? It was always difficult, from the start. From the start, you didn't want to be touched. Remember? Splendid isolation! You wanted to be marble, slate, glass, chrome: anything but flesh.

Until you saw Sir Gold that day. Split open evermore.

FOR INSTANCE (here comes a transmutation of Ovid):

A tough girl strides through the forest, a girl who'd be made of wood if she could be. She doesn't want anyone near her. She's being watched. She doesn't know. Pacing through huge green leaves she brushes aside, she's stalking something elusive. She has on clothes, of course, she isn't naked, but her dress is hiked up so high to stay out of her way that with each stride (he's watching from behind a tree) the cloth flicks enough for him to see the dark moist shadow of what he wants. He's not an animal, exactly, but saliva slides into his mouth and he swallows, licks his lips. When he first saw her, a moving glimmer in the green while he went about his dirty business in the trees, he stopped—something hurt his chest. Something he'd never felt: a rip. His eyes haven't shifted from her since, and although he'd deny it, what he feels—his gaze sliding up her thigh, over the soft cloth with those gentle swells and swayings inside, then dipping as far as possible through the shadowed arm-hole, slipping up her neck slick with tropical sweat—what he feels is a lust rooted as much in groin as teeth, the lust of the hunt. He swallows again, salty, rubs his lips.

He wants to get all of himself inside her. Tongue, teeth, nails, cock. Not hurt her, not exactly. Or if he does—well, that's not his intention.

She's reached the pond. He's been willing her there because that will make it easier. That will show she wants it herself. And now—will she do it? She seems to be thinking. She raises an arm and breathes in her own smell.

Gamey. He can smell the tang from here, he can almost taste her. Oh, yeah. She'll go in. And once she does . . . In his skin his knees turn liquid.

She unbuckles her belt, shrugs the dress loose. Before he can breathe she swivels free of the cloth: a pale shoulder, doe-white haunch, breast so quick he's blinded.

Black dazzles his eyes. His toes dig into the soil to spring—

A message: my mother. Disorienting to be on the balcony, surrounded by Miami roar and warm blue, not in lusty woods.

Darling, she wrote. *Settled back in? Working on O?*

Could see her aim a knotty finger at each key.

Yes! Will call tonight before your Ambien.

Cracked knuckles and looked back at the Latin, book held open with a binder clip. Then looked over at Costa Brava. No naked man today. But in the top-floor gym a man was running in place, staring west through a wall of fogged glass.

—she's running already, naked in boots. Leaves and twigs slap at her arms and tear her hair, but she pulls free just before he can grip her hips because he's that close—he can smell her and almost lick the sweat sheening her back—

Another message:

So you're back in Miami.

One of the gin-drinking old boyfriends. Worst one: the Devil. I knew him when he was a nasty nineteen and got to know his nastier entrepreneurial self on the recent tour of old boyfriends. One who enrages me, but not enough that I won't stay at least a little in touch.

In case.

In case I need someone to send me a message.

He's usually good for that.

Yep, back in Miami.

How glam. I hope you fucking have fun down there. Maybe you'll finally find what you want.

Cracked my knuckles again and stared at the bay. A party boat foamed by, beat bouncing over the water. Two girls in neon bikinis danced on the prow. Almost dusk. Three parrots rushed past the balcony, shrieking.

But now I could smell him. Warm gin-vapor rising from his skin in a hotel somewhere, a big bed with too many pillows, long cloven fingernails pressed in my flesh. But he was so poached that when his purple eyes squinted at me he saw not the present version of me, over which a few decades had run, but a version that was still nineteen. An aspect of him I liked.

FOR INSTANCE (nothing to do with Ovid, exactly):

In the Devil's car a year ago, driving somewhere that would take a long time to reach, he squinted not quite in my direction, one long finger on the wheel, and said:

I loved everything about you when we were nineteen and you would have nothing to do with me. How you walk and talk and look and laugh and sit and look at people and think. Do you hear me? Everything. I'm telling you too much. I should stop telling you all this. It only gives you more power.

Well, maybe.

Did I notice he was the one driving?

Months later, when in exchange for all the power he gave me I'd given him all he loved, in an airport, spotting friends from home, he spun and strode fast from me to them, arm swinging forward in greeting. He did not turn his black-coiled head when I passed; his eyes took care not to know me.

Fucker, typed my thumbs to him.

Fucker, fuckee, said myself back to me.

So who told you to climb on the shark?

OUT BACK TODAY, two of the hot tubs bubbled. In the first a man with threads of gray hair on a barnacled skull held a leg to the jets, face fixed in excruciated pleasure. In the next a withered woman floated with her eyes shut. By the rail overlooking the dock were two men in scrubs and, between them, the Mummy. Strapped in a wheelchair fitted with bottles and stalks, his hair a white cloud, eyes shut, mouth open, chin propped up by a metal brace. He was probably awfully handsome once, is still a handsome ninety. He hasn't been conscious for a very long time.

Over the cracked concrete to the pool.

Was on my sixth lap when Fran rolled out. She is ninety-nine and enormous. She had on a white robe, orange one-piece, and pink bathing cap, and her face is square with a complex, cragged topography. When she and the aide pushing her got near, Jorge dumped his towels and came to help lower her in.

Once in the water, she became queen of the sea, surveying her surf. She shook a hand for her aide to give her a snorkel and mask, fit them on her head, turned, and started motoring around the shallow end. Slow circles, her back a floating isle.

I timed my laps not to collide with her circles, but she's strong as a ship and circled so steadily she created a gyre, and I got caught in her current and swerved. Was getting my footing when I saw her planted nearby. She'd taken off her snorkel and mask and fixed me with a glittering eye.

Guess what, she said.

What?

I've lost almost everything. Both breasts, a hip, my hair, a kidney, and another piece I forget. But you know what?

What?

I don't give a damn!

Good for you!

Nope, she said. I'm ninety-nine and don't give a goddamn. Hell with it all. She looked at me hard, grinned without teeth, adjusted the snorkel, and pumped on.

Floating in the cracked hourglass pool . . .

With Fran's lost parts and a barnacled man and the Mummy.

Stop it! wrote K. *You are NOT in a retirement home.*

Might be just the thing.

NOT SURE I'VE mentioned the deadline for Ovid: twenty-four verse stories in a hundred and one days. Lots of money in work like this, I can tell you. Sort of translation, but only to start: am changing his stories around. I don't think Ovid of all people would mind.

Trans-ferre, tuli, latus: the kind of pattern you can't shake from your head if this is what you've fed it for thirty-plus years.

Conjugations, declensions. Also lyrics.

A song starts in my head, plays in a loop for weeks, won't stop until a new one knocks it from orbit.

But I believe those songs tell me things, floating to my inner ear from a deeper, Delphic self.

Maybe tomorrow, maybe someday, you'll change your place in this world.

This one I heard for years, until I finally left my death-in-life marriage in Deutschland, and the song magically stopped.

Had the lyrics wrong, but still, they helped.

Anyway.

Spread my blue towel on a lounge chair, settled upon it, put glasses on nose, fixed the Latin open with a black binder clip, splayed the dictionary on the concrete.

—She had no chance of running away from that hunter, and when she realized this, she changed tack: she caught a trunk, skinning her arms, shut her eyes, and screamed silently but so intensely that the waves of her will went down through her loins, legs, and feet and into the soil, and it was the soil that saved her. Her ragged toenails she'd only ever cut with a knife dug into the fallen leaves and the earth and latched to rocks way deep, and meanwhile such strange things were happening to the rest of the girl still overland! The skin she wanted no one ever to stroke or nibble or lick grew hard and cracked, the dry places at her knees and elbows whorled and stiffened, and her wrists grew long and thin and suddenly split, twiggy fingers reaching up toward the sky, and now so happy, ecstatic, she threw back her head as her long dirty hair metastasized into leaflets, and she had just enough time to think, I am losing all the parts of myself but becoming what I am, when the wind took the words from inside her mouth and they rustled into air.

Put pencil in spine, rolled over, and stared at the sky.

The sky here is so voluptuous, if you're lying on your back on a soft warm towel, letting the world just spin you.

You can keep climbing deeper into that gassy, dark blue.

What are you singing me now, blue ions?

Framed a square of potent sky with my hands.

But—small lump on my index finger. What? It didn't use to be there. On the knuckle, which I wiggled—stiff.

Silhouetted against the sky, in fact, the fingers all looked knotty. The skin looked downright *whorled*.

Well, good.

Head tilted back, I could see clear up the building. And exactly then the thin white-blond woman came out on her balcony. I flipped over fast to see better. She stood by the railing, gazing out. Then disappeared, and reappeared farther down than she'd been the other day. *Deliberate*. She reached out far, opened her hand, again let something fall. Then peered down to see where it landed.

Experiment?

After a minute I couldn't stand it and hurried barefoot along the cracked path between the gym windows and the low concrete rim that holds back the paradise jungle, to where it must have fallen. Poked at the leaves: nothing.

I looked up the building, up the thing's path—and there she was, all those stories above, looking down at me. We gazed up and down at each other, like I was her reflection, or shadow.

FOR INSTANCE (also not Ovid, exactly):

There was a girl in college who ran. A real runner, yeah, but this was more: she was running *away*. She wanted no flesh that wasn't muscle, and then she wanted her running to eat the muscle, too. That really made her eyes glow. Make me bone, those eyes said. Something so hard no one ever gets in.

Long wild chestnut hair, the sort you can easily see turn into twigs.

A so-called boyfriend of mine with sad eyes had an awful thing for her. She let him touch her once, he said, he almost managed to get her in bed, but that was more than she could take. She ran. From him, other men, everyone. You'd see her pale legs flitting outside the windows of the eating clubs, down the tree-lined streets at night.

Someone must have fucked her up, he said, staring at her hard. Somebody really screwed her.

Maybe, I thought. Or maybe she just doesn't want to let anyone in. What's wrong with that? Who made it obligatory?

Porosity: some have it more than others.

Say, girls.

You have a hole, a boy said to me when I was eight. He and another had cornered me with their bikes against an alley wall.

You have a hole, he said, that I can put my thing in if I want.

For fuck's sake!

That boy's bike crashed to the ground.

MY FRIEND S has just typed me his opinion:

Boys look at porn from the time they're nine. Girls are only body parts.

Mﾟ BUSTER PUDDLES today. Spending a lot of time wiping; knees are getting bruised.

Went outside to paradise—who would not be ecstatic here! How could your heart not flood with solitary joy when walking on the blistering concrete and beholding the hot blue sky and hot green grass and flowers so red they flame your eyes and all that milk-green water? Sometimes there are only depths and depths of dizzying blue up there, but mostly there are heaped white dunes of clouds, sheets and wedding cakes and tire treads of clouds, fata morganas in the sky.

Was brave this morning and left the building not one of my favored back ways, via dock or garage, but boldly through the lobby, past the doormen who love to know who's doing what, past the valets who sneer at my Mini and at the groceries borne home in my bare arms if I've dared venture carless into the tropics to shop. Walked through the revolving doors, past the burbling chlorinated fountain, down the swooping entry ramp, past the row of green fronds and scaly trunks and more girl-trees diving into the ground. Five of them, with silver-pink bark, slim torsos rising from the soil and splitting into long satin legs with tender dark clefts between. They look like naked preteen synchronized swimmers, plunging into the mulch.

Not sure they got away from whatever chased them, with their poontangs eye height and bare, though.

Girls! Close your legs right now, you fools!

To get to Publix, you follow Island Avenue around the oval park, from my building (Nine), past Costa Brava, Sixteen, Belle Plaza, the Venetian, then walk over the last causeway bridge to Miami Beach.

In the water are always needle-nose fish—and, gliding below them today, a ray. A spotted eagle ray, I think, having memorized one once and hurried home to consult my *Audubon Field Guide*. Undulating leopard wings, blue light wavering upon them.

What a place, where you see something like this on your way to buy milk.

Enough to make you forget your chronic life concerns.

Almost.

Just then a Jet Ski boy with a girl stuck to his back swerved by. Engine scream, arc of spray, the fish shot off, the ray glided down into silty dark.

Landed a curse on the pair with my eyes.

Walked over the bridge, past the marina, along a shady block of restaurants and bars, to Publix, which looks like a silver space-shell and is full of porn stars and fabricated beauties strolling the aisles in shoes not made for human feet. Their silhouettes seen from the coffee aisle, down near the illuminated fruits, are extreme. Their natural predators prowl the aisles, spying around boxes of soup.

During the last hurricane, when electricity was out all over the Beach so there was no AC, they say that in the fancy buildings lining the bay the porn stars all went nude.

The sort of statement you can believe.

Like:

You could be a courtesan, as Sir Gold said to me.

He looked like he was actually *thinking*, those hazel-green eyes concerned, proposing what I might try next, now that he was done with me.

Not that I knew this yet, lying naked in his sunny bed, with no desire to leave.

Anyway.

Yogurt, cookies, kale, cat food. Diapers. But no one makes diapers for old cats, only puppies, which I don't understand, so after a while I wandered over to the aisle of baby things. Happy yellow, blue, pink, dimpled bottoms, sweet plum mouths. I found diapers for babies from two down to zero, almost small enough for a skinny old cat. The newborn diapers were a better deal than the ones for dogs, and I was reaching for a packet and feeling golden light sift upon me, feeling a transformation—when I realized the problem of the tail. Returned to the puppy diapers: not cheap.

Shedding money galore for diapers plus litter plus cat food plus pills for both seizures and thyroid. If I drowned Buster today I'd have three hundred dollars a month for my mother.

I *have* taken care of him for eighteen years.

Time to go!

It's been grand!

So long now!

No no no. I'd *never* drown my baby baby baby cat.

Had just checked out and was shouldering my green Publix bags when—oh, no. Par-T-Boy.

Haven't mentioned that there are deadbeats not only north but south: the distant, historic, alluring ones far up I-95, and new ones I've met down where 95 ends.

Par-T-Boy was standing at the cash register about to pay, with five people behind him, when he spotted me and came toddling over, six outraged faces watching. He shrugged, cared not. He's spent so much time in Miami's sonic nightclub scene that blitheness rings him, and the words in his mouth seem to have been blasted apart and re-fused to form a marbly language hard to understand. He owns a bungalow on one of the Venetians and hopes to be a magnet for luscious females, but as soon as they see his front yard, with broken ceramic frogs and ravaging weeds and smashed tiles fallen from the roof, they spin on their Manolos and canter away, and he stands there laughing, bereft.

S'you're back, he said, as the cashier waved her hands behind him.

Yep.

Th'man? he said. Lovoyurlife? Nah? Didn wanyou?

Shouldn't you go pay for your stuff?

He grinned, strands of hair sliding over his eyes. Toldju, he said.

Told me what?

He fluttered his hands. Guysr worthless, he said. Cept me.

Forehead and wrists dripping in the violent sun as I trudged back with my bags, decided I could not face the valets so went around to the side to see Tina in Receiving. I used to think it best to go out in the middle of the day because then, though hottest, the sun is highest, which means that, given that your shadow clings to your feet like a tiny dark puddle, the only parts of you struck by sun rays are the shoulders and head. But after reeling home stupid nine times at midday, I finally ordered a hot-pink UVF parasol on Amazon. The pinkness I hope will camouflage the comedy of walking around sun-bright Miami with an umbrella. I was hoping it had arrived and also wanted to know what Tina in Receiving knew about the problem with the pool.

She works in a small dark room between the Dumpsters and entry to the freight elevator and garage, and has braids of black and gold coiled on her head, rhinestone appliqués on her fingernails, and crosses and holy cards taped to the walls, among piles and shelves of packages.

Oh, yeah, she said, they're always saying something about that pool deck. You haven't been here long enough to hear it.

It's true? It's leaking?

Oh, it's leaking. Everything's leaking. You know this is an old building. Everything here is *old*. Pool, koi ponds, all those planters. Go look at the underside of the pool, she said, down where it hangs into the garage. They say that if they don't do something *soon* someone will get sucked into the pool's filter.

Really!

Won't happen. Hasn't yet. But could. They say. But that's the kind of thing they do say.

Who?

Oh, you know, she said, and zipped her mouth.

Went from Receiving into the garage, underworld of cars, columns, puddles, dripping. How had I not noticed when I rented the place? Where had my *brain* been? I walked in the dimness to where the pool's deep belly hangs down among cars. Stalactites shag its underside, stalactites made of the chemicals Jorge's poured into the water for years, the chemicals that have slid from the skin and hair of swimmers, all of it leaching through the concrete and dripping for two decades down here until it's a grotto, water sliding from the mineral shag even now.

As I turned toward the grated glare of outside, a slim figure passed. Light slanting through the grate struck her and made her glow like a candle, that floating floss of white-blond hair. She couldn't see me in the dark, but when she turned I saw that she could be my mother, or me. In her thin straight back and large gray eyes seemed a wild determination.

Hi, I said, as she pushed the button to crank open the grate.

She startled. Oh, hi. Her voice was rough. I didn't see you. It's so dim down here. But then *here* it's so bright. I don't know. I just didn't see anyone. Well, so long, she said and passed through the lifted grate.

Her long skeleton legs carried her out until she turned west on the Venetian Causeway.

Concrete = WATER + AGGREGATE + CEMENT

Aggregate = crushed limestone (for example)

Cement = powdered (e.g.) limestone

Limestone = calcium carbonate from skeletal fragments of marine organisms such as (for instance) coral

NOW THE MOURNFUL LAWYER has made contact. *Dine with me*, he says.

Another southern deadbeat.

Or not a deadbeat, that's not right, just one of the ones who make me go dead.

He's always driving somberly up and down the causeway in his boatlike car, so if I say no but dare go for a walk he might see me there refusing to dine, and then there'll be long, hurt messages.

The look and sound and smell of him—he's like one of my mother's men from the seventies, the Parents Without Partners men, the hopeless Al Anon men, the men who'd roll up in old white Cadillacs or battered vans for a few weekends to take her out once her husbands had gone, cologned and haunted men (Cadillac), or wild-eyed and briny men (van). The Mournful Lawyer is their kin, their age and as dusky and fragrant, cheeks that are fallen, riven. He drives a funereal Impala, is hard of hearing in the passenger-side ear, furrows his brow if you try to inspire in him a different point of view. His cases involve terms I cannot comprehend, never a word not abstract.

Just plug your nose and do it, says K. Important to get out, get exposure.

Soon he is laying out the plan for an early-bird dinner at a place very quiet and cheap and far away. Google Maps says forty-two minutes even without traffic.

Impossible to focus on O with this looming. Started going out to the balcony with binoculars to see how cars were moving west on the MacArthur Causeway at five o'clock. Slow. By five thirty—what was this?—they had nearly stopped.

When I came down on time he was already waiting with arms folded, his long face in folds of discontent inside his car's musty depths. A raindrop had fallen so he'd taken the precaution of rolling up the windows, air-conditioning blasting thick former scents, windshield fogged with breath.

He leaned over to kiss my cheek, dry lips peeling apart.

Off we went.

So tell me, he said. How have you been.

Well—

Let me tell you first, he said, what I've been working on. I think it will interest you.

He paused, summoning power.

And spoke, but I couldn't begin to tell you what he said as the land of living passed us by. The Impala moved down the ramp, along Island Avenue, past the oval park, and turned right—

Wait—you're not taking the Venetian?

His shoulder cringed and he pursed his lips. The toll, he said.

(Dollar twenty-five.)

There's a Heat game or something, I said. I could see from the balcony the MacArthur's blocked.

Long furred hands clasped the wheel tight.

There is not a Miami Heat game, he said with a hard patient smile. It is not basketball season.

Well, a concert or something. It's blocked.

I've already turned in this direction, he said. So we will take our chances. Besides, this will give me enough time to explain—

And that's the last thing I remember.

LUCRETIUS AND THE atomists before him saw human senses like this: tiny semblances of people and pine trees and oxen and so on were always flying from their source-objects through the air, and if they struck your eyes or nose or ears, you saw, you smelled, you heard that thing. But to have your sensibilities deeply stirred, to be smitten with erotic love—only the rarest semblances could slip through the fine pores of your soul and smite you with *that*, infect you with desire.

The opposite of erotic love: every pore you own, squeezed shut.

W ELL, IT'S GOOD to be out among people, said my mother when I called her after my early-bird dinner and she was still fresh from her own.

Maybe, I said. Anyway. How's the research?

About what?

You know. Your plan for the next stage.

What next stage?

For god's sake. Your dizziness, mother.

It isn't dizziness.

Your loss of *labyrinthine* function, the fact that one day you're going to fall. And not be able to get up!

After a moment she said, Maybe I just don't want to think about it.

You don't say.

What about *you*, she said. Getting anywhere?

With what?

Your research. Your Ovid.

Yes, I said. Of course I am. I am someone who gets things *done*. Every day I type out thirty lines of Latin and turn them into something else. Ovid and I are locked at the hip.

Well, good, she said. I look forward to seeing him.

You know, I said, it might help if you thought of it like going to college again. What would be a fun place to go?

She was silent and I hoped she was thinking. Then she said, That just doesn't make sense.

Well, I have done both research and math, and it'll be Sunrise, that's where she'll go, seven miles from her house. She will *not* live with me, she says: Miami is too hot. She can't live on Meals on Wheels forever, or the fancy foods I sometimes have delivered. And the guy I found to bring in the paper and hose the deck and fix the dryer turns out to be bipolar, plus he smokes secretly in her rec room. No. Sunrise is sunny, people play Scrabble, a lumpy old Labrador roams around to be petted. I do the math often now as I walk or swim, something to add to the menu of counting: how much she'll need and how much she has and the difference between them and what must be done.

What must happen most: this pool must not be demolished.

Swim, TRANSFORM thirty lines of Latin, walk the Venetian Causeway at dusk. Living the life: that's me.

Have to avoid this wicked sun, which mottles my chest. The pink parasol has come, but I don't have the nerve to carry it at sunset. I've found that if you walk with a palm frond or large sea-grape leaf angled right, you can ward off the worst of the sun's late rays, and if you angle it higher you can also avoid the looks of those walking past who are amused by your freakishness. Why be in Miami Beach if you don't like the sun?

Yeah, well, we all have our stories.

Each evening I head out, either the back way down the spiral steps to the dock, or through the grates of the garage, or the front way through the revolving doors and past the chlorine fountain, out to the pink sidewalk ringing the park. Turn left into the searing late sun over more pink sidewalk, and I don't know why the sidewalks are pink although I have looked it up and even read that there's a secret recipe for that hue. Powdered skeletal fragments of (for instance) coral? Then past the subpar Morris Lapidus building, past the Standard across the way, over a low bridge to the green verge, over the drawbridge to the other green verge, over more water to Rivo Alto Island, then Di Lido and San Marino. Venetian names, sort of. Why Venetian makes sense when you walk over a bridge and milky green swells wave along an island's bulwark. Especially with kelp swaying in the wave, a boat's beak bumping the wall.

Romantic fockin' Venice.

Where I lived a few months with the tall black-haired architect who had long trembling hands and a spot in one eye, a spot that struck me as solar.

Like everyone, a liar.

I'd known it going in, regarding his adventures with women before me.

But—*me*, too?

Could it *be*?

We'd laughed about his past deviousness, and he'd shaken his dark head and been amazed at himself and his prodigious deceits, describing the strategies, how he'd tell his current girl of course he'd go fetch the milk she wanted for coffee so he could sneak off to phone the new girl. Even though I knew all this, it *still* came as a surprise.

In my case, it was bread.

And actually, it was me who was sent out for bread, so he could make the phone call from the comfort of our Venice apartment.

I see him lolling there on the bed, long brown legs slithered out from his parted black silk robe. Probably running a hand through peppery hair as he gazes toward the window thinking, *Ah, Venezia.*

Anyway.

It's the kind of thing you can figure out with a phone bill and suspicion.

A month or so after the fact.

Scusi, dov'e un panificio?

The lyrics in my head all that time, had I been paying attention: *Why'd ya do it, she said, why'd ya do what you did?*

Catalogue of comical disasters.

Mind like a museum of them, those men's bodies cast in postures of crime.

There *he* is, on our Venetian bed on the phone. There's the Devil, in the airport charging hard the other way. There *you* are, too, beloved Sir Gold, bidding me be a courtesan.

And others.

I might also have committed some crimes.

Fine: those who think so can put me in their museums.

Venus, meanwhile, clear and bright in the sky!

Like Marilyn Monroe, dancing in that funny red boat.

On both sides of the Venetian Causeway young people display their lovely bright or dark flesh as they run, cycle, skate. Not always but this evening the man whose arms and chest are dense with blue tattoos ran by. He had earbuds in and panted too violently: couldn't hear how loud he was, I guess. A woman jogged past in supershort shorts, with model legs and designer breasts and braided black hair swinging like beads. A man peddled near and wobbled wild when he got to her, yowling at her behind.

Yo mami mami mami!

Mamacita!

Ai.

I walked fast toward the sunset, counting steps. I understand that counting's a symptom but knowing this won't stop me. The number of steps, boats, balconies, strokes, lines of Latin, pages.

Also, I suddenly thought, days since I've had sex.

No matter what your mind wants, no matter what it's resolved to do, Mr. Body still makes trouble.

Thirty-two days is the answer. Ever since Sir Gold.

Solitary pleasuring does not count as sex.

What about atrophy? Does it count against that?

A word my mother whispered to me once. She'd been at the gynecologist's, and when he stepped outside she quickly swiveled her chart: *vaginal atrophy,* in his blue ink.

Started doing kegels as I walked. Something new to count. Now this would be a full-body workout: FitFlops for legs and behind, arm-circling to fight the tender dewlaps hinting from my upper arms, kegels for submarine muscles. I found it easiest to time the squeezes with cracks in the pink sidewalk. Hold tight for ten cracks, release for four, tight for ten, and take it to the bridge.

Should I take 'em to the bridge?

Take 'em to the bridge!

In the middle of the bay flows a quick current of sea that looks like a pale green river. Always something floating in it, bottle, coconut, cup. Easier to be killed by a coconut than lightning. Or shark. I always check the coconuts tumbling in the water, hoping one's a head. Ditto palm fronds re shark fin.

At Di Lido, turned left. Each of the Venetian islands (except mine) is an ellipsis or circle with a single ring road running within, along coral-rock palaces or huge white postmodern boxes, nested in explosions of green. Fan palm, royal palm, poinciana, banyan, orchid tree, bottlebrush, mango. To say nothing of schefflera, bombax, coral tree, cycad, fishtail palm, and banana!

Once upon a time, just sulfurous mangroves, manatee nosing about.

Manatee = mermaid = siren.

Look it up.

In the driveway of an enormous white house-box at the end of San Marino were three black SUVs. The license plate on one was HAREM3, on the next, HAREM1. The other I couldn't see but oh, yes, I could guess. Belonging to the owner of a club? Talent agent for women at Publix? Were some of them in that white house right then? Even when those women lie on their backs, their breasts stand up: you see it on the billboards for augmentation.

I walked on, squeezing and counting. Ten hold, four release. Below huge leaves and a cluster of green bananas dangled a long umbilical cord, from which hung a magenta flower, heavy as a heart. Tiny anoles waited in the grass until my foot was about to strike the sidewalk, then ran out recklessly so I had to lurch to save them. Cats lay stretched in white tribes or black atop Ferraris and Maseratis. A pink crab like a hand clambered into a hole on the sandy edge of the sidewalk.

I used to hallucinate severed hands.

At the time of the end of that architect.

Something to do with a stepfather, no doubt. And trust and fear et cetera.

But happily this ended, so I now have no fear of scuttling pink crabs that happen to look like hands.

Headed back east, sun sinking behind me. As I got near the drawbridge, saw an odd silhouette on the grassy verge. A bird: a duck. But a strange one, somehow *exotic*. And big. A big strange duck all alone, gazing north toward the bay. It seemed noble, or sad. A wave of warmth flowed through me. Resumed my pace and counting.

Near a sign on the bridge for NO SWIMMING NO DIVING NO FISHING were three men fishing. They were not hidden at the foot of the bridge, where the grass meets rocks, and one of them glanced up nastily as I passed. A coconut floated by. Not a head. Also a long palm frond, finlike flange slicing the water. Not a shark. Then a man standing on a surfboard.

He wore thin wrinkled trunks and was lean and dark and elegantly muscled, standing on the choppy water beneath the purpling sky, long pole in his hands. He concentrated on his pole and the water, but as he drew near he glanced at the men fishing, then at the bridge, and then his eyes rose to me.

Lightning bolt!

He reached the bridge and, eyes still on mine, bowed his head to go under.

I stood still as he glided below.

Five kegels later, he emerged on the other side of the bridge and rowed into the watery haze.

I saw again the gray eyes, lean legs. Then saw myself lounging on my back on his long wet board, and the water lapping my hips was warm, and his toes let themselves be tangled in my newly re-goldened hair, and I reached languidly up to stroke a strong calf as he rowed, water slipping over the edge of the board and keeping me wetly warm, and it appeared that I was naked, and now he lifted the long oar dripping water and gently touched it to my knee, then drew it up my thigh—

Hot. My face steamed, sweat slicking the small of my back. Turned away from the setting sun and walked back to my sinking old Love Boat.

*A*N ACTIVE FANTASY *life is good*, wrote K. *But I wish you'd find something with a pulse.*

Buster had one. Picked him up, his claws like pins in my arm, long tail sweeping my hip.

When I change his diapers, we sit on the cork floor, and I clasp him close between my knees. He stretches out his skinny black legs, tufts of yellowing white fur on his belly, and purrs and purrs when I wipe him clean. As I fasten the pieces of blue tape at each side, his forepaws knead the air, reach for my chin, and he gazes my way with blind glass-green eyes beneath long white whiskery eyebrows.

So peaceful.

Certain songs I used to whistle to him, back when he could hear.

His favorite was Gato Barbieri's theme from *Last Tango in Paris*. At the first four notes he'd come bounding.

OKAY, AN ATTEMPT to find a pulse. By chance was on the list for a book party last night and made myself attend. It was up on the Beach, by the golf course. Swinging guests. Sure to be *much* interest in Latin.

When there, behaved Germanly, marching right around the room, outside to the patio, and over to the drinks table introducing self to all I met, offering my hand to shake.

Finally a scruffy man stopped me, holding my hand in his hot one, and said, Wait, I know you.

Oh?

He stepped closer, cracked open his whiskey mouth, and tongued a lip to think, peering up and down at me.

Yeah, he said, I definitely know you.

Had slinked my hand from his by now but something—something in that dissolute face, oh, it called to my heart. The snake-slit eyes?

Got it, he said. Your picture. In a catalogue. Yeah. Book catalogue. Same spread as mine. Oh, yeah.

He looked at me now with those glittering eyes, and I realized he might be right.

I'm right all right, he said. Know how I know? Cuz I masturbated to that picture for a week.

Oh, how my heart called to him! Exactly the kind of deadbeat I love!

But sadly (I learned) he was due to marry the following week, and there's only so much of that sort of thing one should ever give or take.

W ELL, IT'S TRUE: you started out knowing what you were made of and knowing you wanted to stay like that—stone—but then out of the blue one day somebody split you, and where you'd been solid now was a space.

The mechanics of this baffle me, even at this late date.

In her heart opened an inconsolable pain, Ovid says.

In another story, it's an unhealable wound.

Same thing. No revirgination.

But then, on the other hand, there are phenomena like this: I came in the building, collected my mail, stepped in the elevator, and pushed the button for the twenty-first floor, when that golden-gray *pinguis* man rounded the corner with his arms full of magazines. I flapped my hand in the invisible beam to keep the doors from shutting.

Thanks, he said. Thanks. Twenty-two, please. But wait—oh—

The doors were rearing to slide shut.

Come on, N! he cried, his head darting dangerously between them.

I'm talking, called a dry voice from the mail room.

In one motion he laughed and shrugged and leapt back out, just before the doors shut.

In the new enclosed silence, I could almost *see* that invisible beam running between him and his wife, the white-blond woman, N.

It was like the shaft of light in paintings, between the girl and the angel come calling. Something inviolable: love?

It hung in the mirrored marble cube as I rose.

I T'S NOT AS IF I don't understand the problem, you know.

Part of the problem, anyway. About climbing on sharks, etc.

Private etiology of failed love.

Starting out, trailing my mother as she sailed her seas, I had two fathers: the real one we'd left far away, and the false one who was right *there*. Daddy distant; stepfather near.

Awfully, awfully near.

Does a person still need to spell these things out?

So the real father was tucked away on the other side of the world and slowly turned to blue ink. *Dear J:* so faint. *Love, Daddy:* so faint! Even if you pressed your nose to the page, no scent remained of his hand.

The other father, though: oh ho. Hot breath of scotch, smoke like thunder around his dark head, jangle of jazz and slamming of doors and quick bright shatter of glass. And the tall silhouette in the doorway, if you know what I mean.

Surely a person doesn't have to spell these things out.

My friend K, though, prefers to.

You've got intimacy issues, she says. *That's why you keep making bad choices. Mm-hmm. That bastard in Venice vs. your sweet help-less husband. The Devil vs. Sir Gold. All the same thing: the awful sexy monster vs. the distant one you'll never have. You're just replicating the childhood—*

Yeah, yeah.

So what I say is: I am no country for men.

What a boy on the radio's singing, however:

Your body is a wonderland.

WITH GOOGLE MAPS you can see not only this Love Boat but click in close to see the hourglass pool. Click even closer to measure it, which I've just done to calculate how far I swim. The pool = eighty feet × twenty lengths = sixteen hundred feet. If I were to swim that every day from when I got back to my deadline for O, that'd be a hundred sixty thousand feet = thirty miles. Could make it all the way south to the Deering Estate if not drowned or eaten first.

I went down to the pool to cross-measure the length by foot, hiding that I was counting as I paced (three feet per pace) the straightest line possible along the pool's curving lip from shallow end to deep. Reconfirmed count by pacing back to the shallow end, which was reckless because the pool was still empty and limpid and the last thing I wanted was to miss my chance to have it all to myself. Fran rolled out the door. I started to panic, but by the time she'd reached the pool steps I'd dropped my dress and lunged in so the pool was mine first.

Watched her descent. Majestic is the word for it, her aide removing the robe from her shoulders: half Venus being born, half *Titanic*. She attaches her bathing cap, fixes the snorkel and mask, stares hard at the water, pushes off.

When I'd done my laps and had just gotten my footing on the edge of her gyre, she came steaming toward me.

Hi, I said.

Hi. She seemed put off but then gathered strength and said, Haven't seen you here before.

Oh, yes, you have.

She stared at me. Well, maybe I have. Okay. But anyway there's something I want to know.

(Put on an encouraging face.)

Do you still have the three Ps?

The what?

Her lips pulled back to a grinning pink cave.

The three Ps, she said. I've given up on 'em all.

But what are they?

Her eyes went wide and wicked as she leaned forward and barked: Plants. Pets. And *penis*!

She fit on the snorkel and mask and plowed off.

A bee was floating by my elbow, wing faintly fluttering. I cupped it in two hands of water and sloshed it on the concrete.

*F*IVE SIX SEVEN eight nine ten eleven twelve one two three four five six seven eight—

SETTLED ON THE lounge chair that gets shade the longest as the sun wheels around the building, although this means my head's by the trash can. Latin clipped open, dictionary splayed.

A pool of water: let's say a spring. Think of those mineral springs in Florida that bubble up from caves. Clear, but so deep—you never know what's down there.

A girl appears. Not the girl who turned into a tree, but the trees she passes might have recently been girls like herself: that's the kind of world we're in. Sighing trees, fingering with green sprigs the air they adore. Their trunks might one day be cut down but will never be fucked, and for this they shiver in relief. This girl walking through them is an athlete, strong and firm and right now, sweaty. It's hot. Her hair sticks to her forehead and neck, and her arms rubbing at either side are slippery—same between her legs. Gnats keep flitting at her eyes. She smells the spring first, and when she sees the gleam, her mouth waters. She sprints, feet in old leaf-dust and grass and then squelching at the silky, grassy rim of the pond. She can't rip off her dress fast enough but there, it's gone, thrown behind her, and she lurches in to her knees. Water! There is nothing better, parting cool before her hands and welling up around her. She ducks under and kicks, bare bottom with its cleft in the air a silly moment, but it feels good and who's there to see?

Well. I mentioned the depths of this pool, those caves. That's where he is. He's been saving his strength for when someone, a girl, might venture in. It has been a very long time. He feels almost hollow with hunger—

. . .

You can see where this is going. Another attempted rape. She staggers out of the pond and runs and streams with panicked sweat and gets so slippery she realizes that's what she wants, to be liquid—no one can hold her that way. She turns into a stream. What had been a sweaty bare girl suddenly dissolves, only a puddle reflecting sky, then sinking, shrinking, sunk, gone.

I put my pencil in the spine of the book, laid it on the concrete beneath my lounge chair, rolled over, stared deep into the blue, shut my eyes.

That's not how O's story actually ends, but I didn't feel like following it. She turns into a stream, but it's a river thing she's been running from, so this won't help. He just turns back into a river so he can flow with her. *Into* her, *through* her—the Latin prefix means it all. Exactly what she did not want.

No skin of your own, he's everywhere, everywhere.

Leaving mud, smudges, scratches, bites, itchy infections between the legs, bruises that blue you awhile but then green and go. These are the things they leave behind. And thoughts that live a long time in your caves. Words, words, words.

Fascist from the architect; *limpid* from Sir Gold. *Poontang, fockin', hil-ah-rious* from the Devil.

Can't get rid of them once they've got in.

Dried riverbeds left at least, waiting to be filled again when the next man-rush rages through.

In the kitchen wall of the house my husband had when I met him, before the grimness of Germany, were termite tracks, dried rivers I could follow and crush with my nail.

And on a spring morning, transparent wings lay scattered on the blue floor, left from the termites' nuptial flight.

I let them lie there awhile, iridescent in the sun.

Still so hopeful, those early days.

Warm sun on my legs now, dark eyelids a-sparkle. From somewhere far came the clang of rope on mast. Also, a leaf blower droning. Breeze ran over the light down of my thighs, the only female-thigh down extant in Miami. As the sun rolled around the building, I could feel the impending bell of warmth before the strong sunlight itself.

A shadow blotted my eyelids.

Hello, said a husky voice.

(The white-blond Echo woman: N!)

Did I wake you? she asked. I didn't mean to wake you.

No, no, just thinking, I said and leaned up on my elbows.

This close she looked even more like a cross between my mother and me—my mother's nose and chin, body more like mine, but thinner, and so erect. A floss of hair, and in that straight back and jutting jaw what seemed like determination: to endure things you could almost see in her large, gray, watery eyes.

I've seen you in the pool, she said. I usually come out a little earlier than you. To swim. Then I like to sit in the hot tub. Boy, are we lucky here. What a place.

Unless they demolish it.

Which they will, she said. One day. A shame but not a tragedy. I keep telling people that. Even though it's the only place . . .

Yes?

Oh, and she shook her head. It isn't interesting. But I have a question. Do you have any pets?

Yes, I said and thought, For fuck's *sake.* I then told her about Buster and his diapers and pills.

Poor little fellow, she said, looking stricken. It sounds like you're taking good care of him, though. But, well, I'm sorry—I tricked you. I lied. I knew you had a cat because I saw you on the causeway walking from Publix with a big bag of cat food. And that interesting pink *umbrella*. So he still eats?

And purrs.

Well. She spread out her thin yellow hands. Well, then he's alive. You'll know when it's time. I've been there. Oh, it's sad, but you'll know when the time comes. Anyway, what I wanted to tell you is that if you need me, I'm here to help. I care for pets. That's what I do. To keep busy. I retired way too early, it was a mistake. I used to be a nurse. I just like *caring* for things. And now I have all this time and— Her large hands opened up arcs of nothing in the blue sky.

Here, she said, and pulled from her bikini a card with a little black image of a dog and cat, her name printed beside it, N.

Now you have my number in case you need me. Or want to walk, or talk, or anything. Call.

So, THE ORIGINAL idea was to be soapstone, wax.

Erotic Frigidaire, you mean, the spot-eyed architect said.

No, I told him. Not erotic.

But the fact that you're telling me this means you want to be provocative. To tease.

No.

But he was right, sort of. Strength has been the goal. First, impermeability. When no go with that, potency: I'll fuck you, yeah. I'll fuck you *up.*

You could be a courtesan.

Oh dear, Sir Gold, didn't you know? My bill—over there, on the pillow.

BY NOON EACH day the sun has cranked around to the pool and blanched my spot by the trash can, so I stagger in dazzled, then shower, lotion, eat an English muffin with butter and Vegemite, and gird myself for the next stage of work.

I was out at my green balcony table, looking up from the numbered lines of words, fixing eyes on the horizon to stretch them, and cracking my knuckles, when I realized I'd been hearing a patter. A drip of water on the balcony rail. Rain? No. Only that corner. In fact all along the rail as well as on the glass were old yellow sprinklings and speckles. As I was putting together these complex associations, a shower spattered my arm.

Hey! Slapped shut the laptop and craned to look up.

A face appeared above me, then disappeared.

I'm getting wet down here!

Silence.

Are you up there?

I must water my garden, a voice called.

Well, can you keep the water up there?

Silence.

Hello?

I shall try.

Thanks.

Downstairs, men were blowing leaves from the gumbo-limbos. Across the bay, an alarm wailed. *There has been a fire alert reported in the building. Please move to the nearest exit and exit the building. Repeat. There has been a fire alert reported in the building.* In the shifting breeze it became: *There has been ... building ...* Blue, blue sky. A boy playing basketball in the court between buildings yelled

Fuck! whenever he missed a shot. At Costa Brava, two young couples appeared on a balcony. All four put their hands on the rail and gazed out and opened their arms to the vista and turned to one another and smiled. Then they raced back in, where two danced, one threw herself on a sofa and pedaled the air with her legs, while the other tumbled fruit into a blender.

You can see almost everything you need to here.

Requiring binoculars only occasionally.

Looked into my own apartment through the sliding glass doors. Straight through to the front door, broken doorbell fixture dangling beside it.

Not much to see in there.

Back to O. Was working on the eleven-year-old girl on the beach, the one O has climb a bull, but not me. She's in a bright yellow bathing suit, digging moats, making grinding noises inside her mouth, only just beginning to have an itchy sense of the future of wanting, et cetera, about to come.

Maybe first check messages.

No messages.

There has been a fire alert reported—

—This itch, she's thinking as she digs, wet sand grains jamming her fingernails. It's like some alien thing crawling inside her. Or like she's about to become some alien thing. Or in fact she wants some alien thing. She does, she realizes all at once. She shoves her spade into the sand and stares at her little girl-mates around her. Oh my god, she thinks, I am so bored. She wants something supernatural, sublime. Last week, for instance, up the beach she found the head of a baby goat. It looked like a conch from far away, but then she saw its tender ears and, closer, the long lashes around its shut eyes. She squatted to study it and delicately dug just enough beneath its matted little chin to know that the rest of the goatlet was not buried below. It's something like this she wants now. Horrific, marvelous, something to crash in from the other side—

The drip at the corner of the balcony was now a shining thread. It wavered in the breeze, struck the rail, and jagged down the glass; a puddle pooled on the tiles.

—Bring something, bring something, bring something! she shrieks in her head to the sand. Spinning, she screams it to the waves, the sky. Break open and bring me something! Make me—

Messages?

No messages.

Buster appeared at the sliding doors. He'd been doing his circumnavigation of the walls, and since the sliding doors are open, he stopped and sniffed the outside air, long white whiskers and eyebrows alert. Gingerly he placed a paw over the sill. Another paw. A lurching scramble, and out. He swayed. Left or right? Right would take him along the sliding door to where it met the balustrade and, if he kept going, the runnel of water. Wouldn't that be a surprise. He wavered: then leaned his right shoulder against the glass and began to creep. The water now fell in a Morse pattern: runnel-drip-drip, runnel-drip.

There has been a fire alert reported in—

—Now she thinks she actually sees something far out in the water. Really? Out there, yes, where the waves smooth out, or maybe it's the other way around, where they start to swell. She puts a gritty hand to her stomach. Yes—something that is definitely not water is out there, white the way the surface of the moon is white, meaning not really, a curved thing, slicing in—

The other girls are looking, too, huddling dovelike, hands
at throats and mouths in girl-terror. Oh, god, do they disgust
her. She stamps the sand from her knees and steps toward the
water—

Pure drip now. Halfway there, Buster stopped. The diaper with its
blue stickers made his little hips so thin, wobbling above his bony
shanks. Almost no skin on those shanks.

—What are you doing! the girls cry. Are you crazy? You can't
go in! It's a—

Three feet from the puddle now.
Am feeling guilty. Knee juddering with anticipation.

—oh, yes, she can go in if she wants. The itch in her is now a
rip, a rip that wants more ripping. She wants—

A long drop slowly formed, not ready to fall. It swayed.
If the breeze surged—
Buster didn't even know if it was daytime or night.
Once a prancing little boy-cat! A brave small kitten boxing
my hand.
Wavering with opaque eyes, skinny hips, in diapers.
He pressed his head to the glass, pushed on.
The breeze lifted—
And water flew and fell and showered his head, streamed into
his eyes, leaked over his fur, his old curled paws.
Wet fur at my nose, nails in my arm.
I'd *never* drown my baby baby baby cat.

Am THINKING:

Maybe too soon to have cat as only love interest?

Maybe not retire just yet?

Because those giddy moments come, they do, those delirious, ecstatic moments when I've had a little to drink and the garlic sizzles and funk plays loud and I dance, I dance to "Pass the Hatchet," I do the bump with the granite counter and spin and bump again, and I think, yeah—I want I want I want I *will*!

Flash images then of men reeling in and out of the place, me greeting each at the door and dancing somewhere, driving full speed, everything moving quick as light, then waving each good-bye again, a superfast imaginary life.

This is what I'd seen in the sky of spinning ions when I arrived in paradise. This idea of how it could be, once I'd left my poor death-in-life marriage and resolved to live the life.

Before setting all hopes on Sir Gold.

When in fact what happened, what happens, is that the numbers change slowly on the microwave clock as I wait for the pasta to cook, again.

TWO

A NOTICE HAS appeared by the mailboxes: there'll be a board meeting this week to discuss the pool. Now everywhere in the building—lounge chairs, elevators, lobby, garage—white heads nod close and whisper, with quick looks around in case someone hears. Millions of dollars at stake, they say, as much as eight million dollars. It's all about concrete and whoever's most connected to the business.

Worst news.

Did the math as I spiraled down to the dock. Eight million dollars divided by three hundred thirty-six apartments (if you say the Tower and Penthouse apartments each count as six) = about twenty-four thousand dollars each. Which my landlord will pull out of me in nasty big pieces I don't even *nearly* have.

Although I might in six years, if I drown Buster now.

Out on the Venetian, then, walking fast among the jogging and cycling panthers and sylphs.

Once upon a time, when you were maybe fifteen, you didn't even want to be seen, and all the same, out you walked, and honks, shouts, maybe even a crash caused by *you* as you passed.

Now, not so much.

Counted kegels as I walked the pink sidewalk by the roiling bay. In it: tennis ball, coconut, raft of shorn grass. This causeway has just two lanes, sociable. High proportion of black BMWs, many scooters and bikes. A very dark man walks its length from a shelter in Overtown to Miami Beach and back each day. He mutters, lurching from side to side on bare feet with horny nails, wild black prophet's beard swinging, ragged pants roped at his waist, ruined bathrobe. He could be forty or sixty, is fit but fetid, and fixes me with a blazing eye but never nods to my nods. On Fridays, other men with long beards hurry east in black hats and black coats. I step quickly out of their path, so as not to infect them with femaleness.

Femaleness I never even *wanted.*

As Hesiod says: Don't touch the water a woman's washed in! Dirty!

Got to the drawbridge as the bell clanged, but one car gunned it and flew through just before the striped gate came down, and the bridge keeper ran out of her little house and shouted. All the other cars, scooters, cyclists stopped, gazed at their cell phones. I wandered onto the grassy verge.

The ways plants break from the soil here! Royal palms like firecrackers, shooting up straight, then exploding, or mahogany trees no sooner rising than dissolving into a shower of leaves and light. Poincianas like gnarled arms, producing canopies of parrot-green feathers and vermilion blooms; Dr. Seuss trees, bare as bones until pink silky tassels sprout at the tips. Some trees bend back, dig a knee into the soil, and travel underground a few feet before bursting up new.

Sea grapes do this: my favorites. Shrub or tree? They have bark like eucalypts and big round leaves, and right now they're producing long dangles of pale grapes. Each dangle lilts like a banana, showing delicate nude grapelets inside. They fall to the sidewalk and are so light and crisp they pop beneath my heel with a perfection that makes me shiver.

Got my own little sea grape to pop in bed in the dark.

When striving against atrophy and all.

You can climb down the verge to the rocks at the water—and there, today, among the rocks and chunks of concrete dumped to create this causeway, I saw a broken Ionic capital. Crouched to be sure. Algaed stone with twin curving ram's horns in the milky green water, like an actual piece of Venice. Planted on purpose eighty years ago? Did a road engineer or a guy on the crew watch it settle in the muck and think, I hope someone will see this one day and know what a marvelous sense of humor and history someone once had, in *Miami*? I looked up at the road to tell somebody, but no one seemed likely. Anyway, the drawbridge bell was clanging again.

A young woman perched on a moped, staring at her phone. Short gold shorts; bare, smooth, slender, long, dark thighs; tall blue high-heeled boots. Behind her, a young man rocked on his bike. He was grinning just seeing her.

Great look! he called. Love the boots!

She gazed back at him placidly, lowered her helmet, revved off.

He still seemed pleased to be behind her, as he pedaled on her trail.

Looked down at my own legs and realized with *impact* that I don't live anywhere *near* the zone of that woman anymore.

I'm a tree, I'm a tree, I've been caught inside a tree.

A couple raced by on a motorcycle, fumes stinking, her hair snaking the wind, his hands gripping chrome horns. Jet Skier zoomed below just as I walked over the grates of the drawbridge: his plume spumed high, nearly wet me.

Draw bridge a head.

Two men walking a breast.

Yeah, we were all young once.

And, also, alive.

Walked on, kegeling and trying to keep count while calculating how many lines of Latin I'd done and how many still to go, because living the life means chalking off days, the sky turning to sheets of scarlet.

On the other side of the bridge, on the grass near the water, was that *duck*. Did it live there? Strange solo silhouette, gazing north toward the bay. I idled and then stealthily walked toward it over the grass, but my FitFlops thwapped, and the duck startled and fluttered away. But did not fly—could not fly? No, one wing was clipped. It flapped into a sea-grape shrub and huddled in the leaves.

Stranded? On this thin strip between salt water and road? Not so bad at night, but *cento per cento* hell in daylight. Surely it ate grass. Mosquitoes? But it looked thin, and what about fresh water? I had a water bottle and found a curved leaf, walked gingerly over to the duck, who was trying to back even deeper into the shrub, poured water on the leaf, set it down, backed away. After a minute it poked out its slim black-and-pink-barnacled head and slurped.

Stranded. Desperate! And maybe it didn't eat grass: it plucked a blade and let it droop listlessly from its beak.

I walked full of fervor toward the Love Boat. Rescue and relocate? Bring water every day? Food. What sort? Seeds?

A thudding came alongside me, and here was an all-but-naked young man, not too tall and nicely fleshed, skin glistening wet. He was so close, I could *feel* that slippery skin in my hands and I tell you I could taste it, taste his wet skin on my tongue all the way up that lissome sleek back to his young neck and then around his throat and up over the chin to lips I'd part—and then I could feel his wet young tongue. His glance fell on me as he thudded past, then it slid away.

So, IMPERMEABILITY never possible. Ditto revirgination.

Left with objectless want.

This idea of being a cell that's originally intact but is then split open and weakened with want is a reductive way to think, I know. But I find reductiveness helpful. Ideas drawn from Ovid's systems of transformation, plus ancient atomism and eighth-grade science.

Positive vs. negative valence, for instance. *Need* being negative valence.

But how about if we convert need to desire?

Positive valence that way?

Potency, even? Can we say that?

Seems to work that way for males.

*S*O HOW'S THE *glam life down there?* wrote the Devil, as I was researching Muscovy ducks.

Super glam! Lots of fun poolside. Bikini getting action!

Happy times for you.

Darling, wrote my mother, *doing fun things? Seeing friends?*

FIVE THOUSAND a month is what she'll need, and selling her house will buy her only five years, even with Social Security. She's got more years in her than that. Ten?

Or maybe we should not sell her house. Maybe I should quit paradise and go rent her house and just *become* her now.

An old painting I suddenly see in the filmy air: *A fallen woman sits pondering her future, her past. Her hand rests on the warm bone of a skull she's set on the table, candle flame tilting with her breath, the intensity of her thought. That ring of light, of consciousness, bells into the blackness.*

Over at Costa Brava, large squares flash and glow in apartments: one shows a car chase; another, a shooting; a third, a man pouncing on an orange ball, the same man pouncing on the same ball two windows over. On one balcony stands a man with his back to the large bright square, looking at a small bright square in his hand.

Living the life, that's us.

Way to the right, a cruise ship has just broken from Miami and glides slowly through the Government Cut. A fragment of lit, spangled city, steaming out to sea.

Got up and leaned over the railing, bending artfully in two. And became N on her balcony, figurehead at the bowsprit.

ANOTHER FORAY for a pulse. You can't say I'm not trying.

This at least had the quasi-benefit of being research for something I need to know about pigments.

Pigment: Pygmalion: don't ask.

Had heard through good old Par-T-Boy of a painter who might help me, a photorealist painter of, it turned out, perfect ladies who were naked except for high heels as they strode among cheetahs in art galleries. Anyway, went to visit his "studio" (living room). Sat politely as he demonstrated on a painting how he blended tones, pointing first at the nether area of one of his naked ladies and then drawing a little circle upon a more focused bit of her groin and then moving his quick little finger in tighter and tighter and more frantic circles over the dream girl's painted crotch until that patch of painted lady was a gloss and his eyes had gone to glass.

The room was AC-dry but I made myself not even lick my lips.

THIS MORNING, went swimming early. N had just stepped from the hourglass pool: a wet animate skeleton in a bikini, hands and head too large. With her hair slicked back she seemed a young dancer, or a quite old one.

After I'd swum, she wandered over in a towel and white hat almost the size of my pink umbrella and asked if she could ask me a question.

Sure, I said, if I can ask you one back.

But wait, she said with her husky New York voice. Didn't I see you on the causeway the other night, over by the water? Sort of . . . squatting? It was almost dark. What were you doing? I hate to say what it looked like. I told P you were not the type to do that on the causeway.

Nope. Who's P?

My chaperone.

What?

Just kidding. My husband. So what were you doing? You looked very *furtive*.

There's this duck, I said and told N about her.

Really? she said. She's stranded?

And alone, which doesn't seem right.

No, N said, her head tilting. How do you know it's a she?

She's smaller and warbles, which is what they say the females do.

Well, it's very concerning that she's stranded, N said. What will she do for fresh water?

Exactly what's worrying me.

Well. Maybe we should try to do something.

I plan to bring water every day. And Grape-Nuts. I can't walk by and see her helpless like that. She's getting thin.

N looked at me for a time, her eyes like deep pools: you could almost see something swimming inside them.

I think that's good, she said. I think that's *good* of you. You care for creatures that need care. This is important for people to do. And when I walk on the Venetian, I'll also bring her water.

But what I really want to do, I said, is transport her to a place with other ducks.

She considered me again.

Well, that sounds like the right thing. Yes.

But I think it'll take more than one person. She's skittish and waddles fast.

N's expression went cloudy. So . . . you want help? You do. Oh, she said, oh, no. I can't. I mean of course I *want* to. Given how I love animals. But any kind of running and quick bending . . . I can't. I have this . . . oh, it's too boring. I have a lot of pain.

She shook her head and put up a hand before I could ask. No no no, she said, it's not worth talking about. Bad surgery, that sort of thing. But anyway.

I'm sorry, I said.

Well. She unfolded her long bone legs and stood up Pilates straight, ribs looking beached, in her tiny bikini. But she didn't walk away. She took off her white hat and turned back to me as I sat with the dampening book in my lap.

But that wasn't actually my question, she said, about you and the duck. And you didn't even ask me yours! Do you mind? It's none of my business. I don't want to pry. But I can't help it. So if I might ask . . .

Yes?

Well, you seem to be by yourself all the time, and I'm wondering, isn't there someone in your life?

The lounge chair was soggy from overnight rain, and wet had seeped into my towel and gone cold. I put my hands on the Latin and thought, For fuck's *sake*. Then looked up at her brightly.

Not just now, I said. But I've got O!

She smiled the slow, sad smile. Okay, she said. You have O. And the cat in diapers. And the duck. Those are your loves. Okay. Maybe that's all you need. Who knows? Maybe that's enough. I don't know. It's none of my business. But wait a minute, she said. What were you going to ask me?

Oh, I said, my face afire, it was just about the duck.

Okay, well, she said. Maybe I'll see you at the board meeting tomorrow.

Yeah, I said. But—

Yes?

I mean, I did have a question.

We looked at each other, and again it felt as if she were the face and I were the pool.

What do you drop?

Her eyes went away. Excuse me?

From the balcony?

Oh, she said, how embarrassing. And she laughed her strange dry laugh and unfolded her limbs and wandered away, that white-blond hair like a halo.

J UST WHEN I was getting some *clarity*, he sailed back into my in-box.

Looked at his name a long, long time.

Counted the letters, again.

Calculated their worth in Scrabble.

Twenty-one.

Each one golden no matter its worth. Golden still, *still*.

Clicked, knowing this would slay hope.

Ahoy! Where are you? Back in Tropicana?

Yes! I wrote fast, denying fury and hurt.

Wrote him about sea grapes, pink crabs like hands, diving trees, duck, and thought hard at the screen, *Leave your stone house, you fool, and bring your dog and come. I am for you, and you are for me. We can live the life!*

Then I went back to polishing the story of the girl with the shark, getting up every ten minutes to nuzzle Buster, going back with fresh hope to the screen.

Finally:

Glad you're happily settled home! Enjoy la vida loca!

And back he trotted to the farmhouse, solo with the dog.

Well, Fury. You know how Fury came to be? A boy-god named Time sliced off his father's penis and threw it out to sea. As the penis zigged through the sky, one end spurted semen, the other blood. Drops of blood hit the sand and sank, and from them spouted Fury. From the froth that foamed and sputtered out of the tip came the goddess of erotic love.

Another version of the birth of that problem.

You've noticed the twinning in these etiologies. Fury + Love; Want Nothing + Want.

Anger and lust.

I can't live either with or without you and don't seem to know my own mind, says O.

Yeah, we all know about that.

NEW MOOD:

A swimming pool, twilight. Let's make it the pool here, the one like a lopsided hourglass. Not dusk but dawn, pearly light. The water is deep, delectable, untruly blue. It looks like a pool of pure color. To touch it would not cause a ripple; you'd dip in a hand and be hued with blue light.

At least this is how it seems to the boy who's just arrived. A young boy, in these stories they're young, that's the point, at the age when . . . Fourteen, maybe fifteen. He has never been touched. A cerebral boy, and in his slim body is a mind intoxicated by purity, by ideas of a pool filled with light. If he could not have a body he would gladly be rid of it; he'd sublimate, slip free. He has not come from inside the building because a boy like this doesn't live in a building; no, he skidded from the sky and loped around the side of the building and triple-leapt the spiral steps, materialized here, out of breath. Now he stands on the lip of pure color. He himself is the color of limestone, fresh living rock just split. What's he wearing? Not much, faded trunks. He stands looking into the blue. Although he knows it isn't really light but water, he wants to will his belief true, so slowly dips his toes, dips until toes touch blue surface, tense light.

And the water—at his touch, the blue water trembles and softly sighs. You wouldn't hear it—this boy doesn't—but all the same, it sighs. This pool, you see, is feminine—

New mood, new stories. I'm moving down the list. From girls running away to what's at work in this one.

Desire.

Potency?

I'll fuck you, yeah. I'll fuck you *up*.

I don't really mean it. Just, please.

W HEN THE SUN had cranked around and flooded the pool with harsh unbearable light, I went in and up. Stepping out of the elevator, ran into the Frenchman who lives down the hall and is squat but stout and emanates heat. He walks fast and hard in shorts, with stocky furry legs and flip-flops, and bellows cheerily at the little dog trotting beside him. The dog likes me and today tried to run into my apartment when I opened the door; the stout Frenchman had to bark at him to make him come back. A few days ago the little boy whose grandparents (Jamaican?) live across the hall also tried to scoot inside. I don't know why. He has a clear and piping small voice, his name is either Brando or Marlon, his hair is a sweet dark tumble of coils, and he looks about three. I had passed him and his mother heading toward the elevator, and suddenly he stopped, pulled free of her hand, and trotted after me back down the hall. His dark eyes were round at my open door, and he seemed hypnotized, drawn by the light.

Come in, come in, I chanted in my head. *Come be my little boy!* The words were streaming from my eyes and he was nearly pied-pipered in, but his mother snatched him away.

—If this boy by the pool had been smarter, yet less brainy, if he'd stepped back and looked, he'd have seen. Those hourglass curves? Of course it was female! And now the blueness of the water—because it is water with the warmth of blood, water that will lap around you and hold you or maybe let you sink—now, at his touch, the blue of the water deepens. Dip again, the water sings. Dip again, please do. He doesn't hear this but nevertheless does it, dips his toe, and strokes the surface, gently, raking a light and delicate swell. The pool, just perceptibly, trembles. It is so tense! And the pleasure of this touch is too . . . too much. When he strokes and dips again, the pool breathes more deeply, swells with need, and then, when he doesn't dive—too abrupt—he sits on the smooth white lip and slowly sinks one leg, then the other, and then, with a wriggle, drops himself to the hips into the warm blue, it does what it wants to: envelops him.

BALCONY, NIGHT. Drinking more than O would like but not nearly enough for me. *Time and again I tell myself I'll stay clean . . .*

The lower sky's full of glittering buildings, the bay's full of glittering boats, the water's full of echoes of both. In the upper sky, Orion tilts along with his belt and starry sword.

Below the sword, in Costa Brava's top-floor gym, two men and a woman run toward fogged glass. They look brave and serious as they gleam and stare west.

Five stories down and two windows over, a dinner party. The hostess gets up from the table and walks from room to room, windows lighting as she goes. Alone in the kitchen, she opens the fridge and assembles things at a counter. Three windows over, the guests lean close, an arabesque of light over their heads. The paintings behind them are deep red, green. She sets small plates on a tray that she now carries back from window to darkening window until the group at the table turn their heads, and she's with them again.

A corner apartment near Star Island is a bordello. This is a fact. A man will come out in underpants, with a cell phone, cigarette, and drink, looking sated as he gazes toward the island where Madonna sometimes lives. Then a bikinied woman or two might come out and lean against the railing, not near him, and smoke. Different women, different men, never a lot of clothing.

Up to the northeast, over the sea, a point of light grows in the sky. Behind it, a smaller point emerges from darkness. Behind this, another, smaller still. No matter when you look at night, always this configuration of swelling stars, as plane after plane flies down the shore and swerves westward at the Venetians.

Inside, Buster leans against a wall, swaying.

No other movement in my place.

No sign of life at all.

Maybe the digital clock on the stove ticking off minutes as they die, here in la vida loca.

Buster isn't even swaying; he's asleep at a slant.

Could stare at the cork floor and imagine swirling ocean depths.

Could look out at the ocean and imagine the same.

Could look down from this balcony to where boys shout *Fuck*.

Could look down down down to nada.

Sudden flare of blue light at my hand!

The Devil.

Might have business in that glam Miami of yours. Working on a deal with the Miami Heat. Not that you want to see me, but. I promise to be nice.

The problem with the Devil is that he was always good at sex.

Had a sudden full sense of his slick lips I used to like to slip my tongue between. And the way his tongue and all shot back, alive. No getting up from that bed.

Had to put down the cell and look at the sky for a minute.

NO, wrote K. *Do not answer that message. Delete it. That man is poison. Your other old deadbeat is heartbreaking but this one is only poison.*

Not a good idea, my thumbs said to the Devil.

Of course it is, his thumbs said back.

THIS EVENING I brought a dish to fill from my water bottle, as well as a baggie of Grape-Nuts. Set dish near the duck's shrub and strewed cereal near my feet. Her black-bead eye looked at this but she didn't move. So I stepped back, and after a moment she waddled out of her shrub, first pecked cautiously at the nuggets, then gobbled. I crouched, balancing on my heels, and watched. When I thought I might touch her black barnacled head and tried, she shivered and scooted off fast. Left her searching for nuggets in the grass and walked the Venetian, timing walk to end when the board meeting began. Then snuck into the Bay Room.

The five board members sat at a long table facing the residents, glass wall of the bay and Star Island behind them. I've never got their names straight, although I've seen them in the lobby and elevators looking stuffed with import. The chair was droning into a microphone about contractors, as people in the audience muttered and stirred, when in the middle of a handout, Lino came in. He wobbled forward in his white linen shirt and white pants and white hat. He got halfway up the aisle, then stopped and waved his cane.

You, Harry! he shouted. You're a crook and a thief and you know it. Don't anyone believe a word he says!

Lino twirled around unevenly, still shaking his cane. Time for a new board! Call an election!

Lino, said one of the board members into his microphone, Lino, we're having a meeting here.

Same with you, Tom! Liars and cheats, all of you! Call an election!

Lino, said Tom. Calm down.

Don't tell me to calm down! Don't tell me to calm down! You're planning a heist while you're still on top, and if you do I tell you what I'll do—

Lino . . .

—I'll have you killed!

Two of the board members stood up. That's enough, Lino, said one, and then the other was suddenly rounding the table shouting, You get the hell away from my wife!

Lino had veered toward a seated woman with a yellow bow on her head looking fiercely up at him.

You and your wife! Lino said. Have you all rubbed out!

All right, that's it, said Harry and banged his gavel, and in came the head of security, Virgil—his name really is Virgil—who is two feet taller and broader than Lino and very dark, with dark, sad eyes. He cupped Lino's elbow and steered him gently out of the Bay Room.

All right, said Harry.

Then the board went on with its business, Chairman Harry telling us all that was wrong with the pool and garage and koi ponds and jungle, the unsoundness of the concrete, the fact that cracks weren't just in the surface but symptoms of deep erosion, that the whole thing was about to collapse, taking koi and palms and gumbo-limbos and sunbathers and swimmers down with it, and as he spoke, an evil tiny smile on his face, it felt as though a tunnel were opening up and we were streaming into it, tumbling down into darkness, little naked Bosch figures, animals pitched from a sinking, split ark.

Two years of smashing and dust and blistering noise and *nine* million dollars, is that what he said? Did he say that?

I looked for N but couldn't find her among all the white-blond heads.

MY MOTHER WILL not go to Sunrise, she says. Absolutely not. Which is not yet bad news, there being the threat of increasingly negative funds thanks to the pool demolition.

But she will not even visit the place to *see*.

Why should I, she said. I'm not ready.

What about future preparedness? I said.

Future preparedness for what? she said.

For the *future*.

She was quiet, then said, That just doesn't make sense.

Tropical wind blew through the phone.

After a moment she said, I think you should just worry about your own self.

I can't help it! What if you fall? And you're lying there alone and nobody knows!

Well, I won't, she said. I never do.

Like everyone, a liar. Last year, a broken ankle. The year before, a wrist. And the bruises, blooming blue bruises on her forehead, her arms.

Oh, it's just the *Plavix*, she says. Never mind.

She won't even wear that alert thing around her neck. The pendant that'll send in the medics!

What is it like in that skull of hers, or in her hands or feet where the nerves have died? The horizon started tilting and she'd shake her head as if knocking water from her ears, but that made the world wobble worse. Gradually she could no longer feel the world, either: nerves turning to wood in her fingers and toes. Aiming a finger at a key to send out a word, she misses, concentrates, aims again, but it's too much, everything just keeps slipping, the world's forms tilting away. Does she want this now? Want it all to go?

OVER AT COSTA BRAVA, on a balcony on the seventeenth floor, a young woman who always wears vivid clothes has just come out with three other women, two men, a tray of drinks, and drums. They arrange themselves and toast and sip, and as I type right now they've begun to beat the drums and sing.

> *Caught in that sensual music all neglect*
> *Monuments of aging intellect*

(No, they're not singing a rendition of Yeats.)

Below them, darkened windows, just two with big lit screens, one flashing a man in a jungle, the other, two brides tearing each other's spumy dress. In an apartment to the right, three children jump on the sofa, skid on the floor, maypole around a potted palm, no adults in sight. Family probably just flew in from Peru, parents wrecked.

The bordello is dark tonight.

Straight across, though—what's this? A sudden low-lit movement of flesh the colors of an ice-cream sundae: couldn't make it out but the rhythm was clear. Time for binoculars. Hurried inside, got them, switched lights off for secrecy, and my magnified eyes roved across the building until I located the motion. Focused with thumbs: cluster of men. Hard to peel one from another. How many? A lamp gave just enough light—five boy-men, a sectional sofa, zebra-print rug, marble table. Silver wallpaper glimmered with the motions of flesh.

I'm floating eyes, floating eyes, I've been transformed to floating eyes!

Put down the binoculars, set hands on table. Felt them there, warm and taking up living space.

Felt lower self sitting in chair doing same.

Poor old lower self.

Far at sea, beyond Costa Brava and over the bay, beyond the lit buildings on the Beach, in the dark liquid distance: heat lightning. A silent flash, delicate jag at its heart. The sky dark and still for a moment, then another silent flash. Beautiful, each jag and flash at sea, flare dissolving like cloud.

ARE WRITTEN WORDS part of the problem? Translating, transmuting, part of the problem? Did words swim alone in people's heads before writing was invented—I mean, did words exist in silence before writing, or never until they'd been blown past the teeth? Homer, was it different then? Or has everyone always been a private pool of silent swimming words?

S *TILL ALIVE down there?* wrote the Devil.

Well, this is an excellent time for words to stay silent inside my head, not be sent by treacherous thumbs to the Devil.

FIRST THE CLUSTER of young men last night, and this morning: by the pool lay two men on lounge chairs who I *know* don't live here. Obviously guilty, they'd snuck in. Which you can do. You can slink by the basketball/tennis courts over where the fence comes closest to the building but leaves just enough room, slither through to the dock, and then casually spiral up the staircase like any civilian resident, because the lock has been broken for years. Virgil shakes his head and sighs at it. These men were the breed who make women invisible, but this made them easy to watch. I was swimming, and each time I clutched the rim to gasp, I let my invisible binocular eyes stray over to spy. Between laps one of the men got up lazily and disappeared into the men's spa while the other smoked, looking up now and then toward the door to the spa; the first one came out and strolled back to his friend. They said something, and the other got up and walked to the spa. I swam three laps and was in the deep end clutching the rim and panting when he came out. He looked altered, loose in the hips.

Lots going on in the spa, he said to his friend, who looked at him, grinned, shook his head, got up, and went back in. The other one lay down, lifted a knee, lit a cigarette, let his free hand drop.

Nasty, part of me thought, winging and frogging fast to the shallow end. Hmm, thought another part. What if I could go into the spa after swimming, all wet, with my blood warm and rushing, and maybe not turn on the light but glide over the tiles in the dark and rise up the altar steps to the hot tub, and maybe it's already bubbling and dreamy, and once I've stepped in the warm water and wiggled down and am getting steamy and expansive I discover, oh! another body in there with me?

I leaned on the cracked lip of the pool trying to decide: man or woman in the tub? Usually it would be a man at this point in the fantasy, but this was the women's spa, and the idea of a woman with wet slippery breasts seemed good.

Plunged on.

Yes yes yes, a warm, wet body is in the bubbling water behind me, and hands suddenly find my hips and pull them to him, okay, sorry, it's a him, and his legs come up on either side so warm and strong, and he pulls me to him and then has more hands and they each rise over my belly and just under my breasts and linger, as I lean forward to get my breasts to touch them, and then the hands understand and decide to tease and hold themselves out just in front of my nipples in the warm bubbling water and then glide by . . .

So HERE'S A new question: do I have a choice, at this point? Not counting, of course, the Devil.

Floating and floating in the hourglass pool . . .

Lotion and sunblock and skin cells of me, seeping into the water, sinking through the pool's deep belly, dripping down into the cave.

Another etiology, Hesiod again: he puts Desire in the world at the very start, created only moments after primal Void.

Aloneness did not have a chance.

JUST AS I GOT to the part of a story where a beautiful boy who wants nothing (Narcissus: a.k.a. *you*, Sir Gold) dissolves into his quicksilver self, water splashed my balcony table. Not even in the corner where it had drizzled last time, where I'd set the corn plant I found in the trash room and rescued, a corn plant that still had a single live leaf so was not yet completely dead and thus deserved, like many deadbeats, my love.

I slapped shut the laptop, glared at the balcony above, went inside, stalked through my apartment and down the hall, took the stairs two at a time, and knocked on the door of that lady: silence. Went back downstairs, wrote a note, ran back up, and slid it under her door, panicking that she'd swing open the door just then and charge me with cowardice. As I hustled back down the hall, N rounded the corner.

Well hi, she said. Were you coming to see me?

Told her about the water woman.

She *seems* nice, N said. She does have a lovely garden on her balcony. But I can understand how annoying that must be. Do you want me to intervene?

(Shook head.)

Why don't you come in, she said. Have some coffee.

(Ovid ticking in my chest.)

One little cup of coffee, she said.

N's apartment, on the other side of the building from mine, looks over the paradise jungle and brilliant blue bay, Monument Island, the city, the ships. I gazed a long time as she made coffee, then was looking straight down all those stories at the greenery and path when N came back.

Tried touching the duck last night, I said.

No luck?

She's fast. I gave her Grape-Nuts, put them near my foot, and she came over and bobbed for a minute, then started to eat, and I was sure I could grab her, but no. She waddled off and dropped into the bay. But even if she got to Rivo Alto, there aren't any ducks there, either. Or fresh water, except maybe somebody's pool. What I realized then is that someone else is leaving her food: by her shrub was a dish of cat food. *Cat* food.

That can't be very good for her.

It's disgusting. Whoever it was left an empty bottle, too, actually a few.

Just tossed?

It looks like they might have brought her water and then left the bottles. So I'm going to put a note in one.

N looked at me. A message in a bottle?

Saying *We need to save this duck!* and giving my number.

Well, said N, it'll certainly be interesting to see if anyone responds.

I'm hopeful.

Now this duck is intriguing, she said, but to tell the truth I'd rather know a little more about other things.

I told her about the cluster of men across the way and the men going in and out of the spa.

Well, she said, that's also interesting and does not surprise me one bit. This is *Miami Beach*. But what I want to know, she said, is about *you*.

Told her about my mother and the labyrinthine problem. Then, after nudging, told her about the deadbeat men. Sir Gold, the Devil. Didn't mention husband, much.

N, like K, thought I ought to meet *new* men.

Look at you, she said. You're desirable. You could have . . . all sorts of opportunities.

Her phone rang, and when she went inside, I looked again at the water, islands, city, sky. Up where all those siren ions once sang their song of hope. A pair of pelicans soared by, coasting so close you could almost touch the ashy fur of their breasts, beaks like oily shell.

When N came out again she said, Is it a fear of flying?

I shook my head. Her wing's clipped.

N smiled the slow smile. I wasn't talking about the duck, she said. See? You're too young to even know what I'm talking about. *Fear of Flying*. The *book*. Look it up, smarty. I was talking about you. The unknown, she said. You know. Letting yourself go, all that junk. That's what you're afraid of.

Sure, I said. Who isn't.

Oh, I don't know, she said, sometimes— But just then her face, with its disturbing wide smile and liquid eyes, her face like a beatific jackal, got pulled by that pain inside her. She placed a large thin hand on either side of her chair, eyes focused nowhere.

Okay, well, she said. I know you've got lots of work to do. It's nothing. The usual. See you soon.

THIS EVENING on the Venetian, message rolled up in my pocket, I saw again the runner whose whole body is tattooed, at least the skin not hidden by shorts. Have always thought the patterns were paisleys, but when he passed close, saw they were the seams and striations of red and blue meat—tattoos of the muscles inside.

So as I walked and tried to kegel, of course I thought of "The Human Body": that exhibit of people who'd donated their dead selves to be skinned, preserved, and mounted for view.

It started in Germany when I lived there. Then it traveled all over the world, a caravan of skinless bodies in elaborate poses. Midstride, odalisque, midfuck. I think one peeled body was hitting a volleyball.

It happened to be curated by the husband of my doctor.

And as soon as I thought of it, even the balmy Biscayne Bay air wasn't strong enough to overcome the smell of that waiting room in Heidelberg, the waiting room in the *Frauenklinik*. The other fruitless women, bitter with added hormones and subtracted caffeine, sat in wooden chairs against the walls and waited, the floor muddy, smell of old wet stone and must. Every so often a door in the corner would open and a voice would cry *Die nächste,* and the next woman would get up and look back at us waiting and go into a lit room for blood to be drawn, then into a dark room to take off her pants and lie back and let the probe be jabbed in and tooled around to see if any grapelets were growing. We were to get up and go in the order we'd come, and it was our job to know this order, so each looked up fast when a new harried woman appeared at the door, to be sure she knew her place. I'd memorize each woman's face, look at the other slumped waiting bodies, and gradually think of the people who'd donated their dead selves to my doctor's husband, the room slowly blurring into a tableau of peeled bellies and heads.

By now I'd reached the green verge on the other side of the drawbridge, the duck standing in her station, gazing bravely north at the bay. As soon as she hears my FitFlops now, she starts waddling to our meeting point by the sea grape. I strewed Grape-Nuts and poured water into the dish, and as she shucked her fear and darted close to begin eating inches from my foot, I tried again to touch her—fingers nearly on her shiny black feathers—but she flapped away, affronted. Okay, okay. Under the shrub was a plastic bottle; I slid my message inside and tied a pink ribbon around the neck.

Hello, whoever is feeding this duck—please call! We have to save her.

At the next island, on one broad square of pink concrete, two tiny anoles wriggled entwined. At my bad-luck footfall, they scratched away quickly into the grass.

GOOD NEWS! The labyrinthine-brain coral continues to live, down by *Paradise Found*. I squatted in the sun for a time to watch it waver through clear green water.

All those coiling passages. Brains, intestines, inner ears.

Female passages, too.

Hysterosalpingogram being a good, if sad, way to see them.

Uterus-salt-dye-picture.

Which I've been thinking and thinking about again, ever since the Human Body ran by.

You lie on your back in a room lit by little lights on machines, same room as always or maybe an earlier dim room in another city or country, because this went on an awfully long time, and you watch as the doctor's hands say *Go,* and up inside you flows the ink, branching in ever tinier tributaries, like a water land shining in the dusk. And if the ink travels far enough, you know that this at least is not the problem.

In the museum across the street from our apartment, the Zentrum für Kunst und Medientechnologie, was a glass sculpture of the viscera of a shark. My favorite thing there. A glassy tumble so large on the scuffed floor in cool northern light that it took time to circumambulate. Its kidneys, liver, intestines, and heart, translucent, fragile, and clean.

AFTER WORKING late last night, needed *out* and went down to the dock. Gazed at the dark glittering bay to the cityscape of red, green, white lights, up to the blowing tropical sky, ripped clouds lit blue by the moon. Then something suddenly came to life on the tallest distant building: a twenty-story dancing girl made of LED lights. I leaned elbows on deck rail and watched her swing her pony mane, wriggle her hips, kick her white boots.

Light-Emitting Diode: like a tiny bright creature in surf.

When I came in at the side entrance by the Dumpsters, where Tina in Receiving has her crosses and saints, a trio emerged from the dark: small mothy Lino and two girls like the light-girl. Their cheekbones in the street lamp were Russian. The girl on Lino's left had blond hair, the girl on his right had red, their breasts the height of his nose. He'd picked them up? They'd picked him? Over his white hat they looked at each other, then each slipped a hand through a crook'd arm, and the three went into the building.

I waited, invisible, by the Dumpsters until the freight elevator had taken them.

Lino lives in the Tower, I happen to know. It's better even than the Penthouse, marked on the elevator panel as T.

I have not yet dared go up there.

I mean, I barely dare come in through the lobby.

A few minutes later the girl-fragrant elevator came back to me, and I rode to my twenty-first floor. And thought about the fact that in the bordello and silver apartment across the way, and the spa downstairs, and bars and bathrooms up and down the Beach, and even in miniature Lino's *tower,* all sorts of sex were waged.

Lay in bed then and stared at the popcorn ceiling in the dark, bones grinding into the mattress.

It wasn't Fury really.

Just Time whetting his knife.

How long can you float in the hourglass pool?

Sudden glow beside my bed:
  So? wrote the Devil. *Ready to deal with me again?*

A NOTICE HAS appeared in the mail room: next week will be elections for a new board.

Lino!

What do you think? I asked Tina.

She looked up from her logbook, braids jingling with beads. I don't know, she said. I just don't. What I do know is that there is always trouble, no matter what board we have. This one we have now? They've been here a *decade*. They will not leave peacefully.

So there will be trouble?

Oh yes, she said, and handed me my box.

Back on the balcony working on transmutation thirteen—halfway through, done with the stories of hunting and running and on to incest and sex-change—water *again* splashed my arm and, when I craned out to see her, my face.

For fuck's *sake*.

No one up there, only drops falling, bright with sun, out of the deep blue sky.

Stalked inside and down the dark hallway and out into the flaring light to the external stairway and up to the twenty-second floor and down that hall until I reached her door and knocked. Nothing. Knocked again, *pounded*—there was a stirring up and down the hall. Her door cracked open: an owlish face with a quiff of hair and eyes that were small and mean.

Come *on*, I said. I'm soaked.

I cannot do anything about it, she said.

What?

I have a garden. A garden needs water. There is nothing I can do.

You can water more carefully, that's what you can do!

I am doing the best I can, she said, and shut the door and locked it.

If your plants were inside, I bet you'd water better! I shouted at the wood.

When I turned around N stood at her door, sunlight flowing behind her.

Oh my, she said.

It's funny, I said, everyone drops things from their balconies on this floor!

Her head tilted, troubled.

I'm kidding, I said. It's just you and whatever it is you do out there and now this *woman* and her water.

Oh, right, N said.

Okay, I said. Okay. How are you?

Oh, and she let her hand and word float.

What do you think about the new board elections?

Well, she said. It'll be interesting no matter how it goes.

They all seem nuts.

Sure they are. She smiled and after a moment said, Do you know what Harry and Tom on the board call you? Professor Mermaid. Because, you know—she spread out her arms—there you are with the dictionaries and all. By the pool. In the *bikini*.

My face must have looked funny because she quickly said, No, no, they're not teasing you, they like that you swim and work hard. They *admire* it. They're *attracted* to you. If you like, you know, I could—

Attracted! I reeled down the hall. Okay, two eighty-year-old men are attracted to me, two men covered with barnacles. But okay, so is the duck. It doesn't mean they think I'm one of them. Do they? *Am* I? Is this how you find out? Patronizing doctors calling you Young Lady, innocent awful children calling you Old Lady?

• • •

Then, in the pool, after five hard laps, Fran stopped in the shallow end and fixed me with her eye.

Hi, Fran, I said.

She grunted. Guess we've met.

Sure have.

After a minute she said, Got a question for you.

(Oh, no: not again with the plants, pets, and—)

You mean the three Ps?

Huh, she said. Guess I've asked you before. So. You still got 'em?

Only two.

Speak up!

Only two Ps left for me, I said, and sent her a swift wave of pool water.

Bet I know which one you don't have. Well, the sooner you're done with 'em all the better. That's what I say. Join the club.

Hold your face *up*! I shouted in my head as I marched on the causeway, fiercely counting kegels.

Go get highlights, wrote K. *I can tell from here the gray is showing. Men don't like gray. Reminds them of their grandmothers. Do it and send me a picture so I know it's true.*

Lucky we've known each other since we were nineteen, wrote the Devil, *so I know silence is how you say yes.*

W ELL, YOU KNOW: the devil you know.
    GIMY, he used to type, for me to figure out.
    First I thought it meant *Get in my yard!*
    He said, Well, not exactly.
    In fact it meant *God, I miss you.*
    Who wouldn't trust a devil like that?
    AIWITSONWY.
    I did enjoy figuring.
    All I want is to spend one night—
    So, yeah, the devil you *know*.
    Medical necessity. Atrophy and all.
    And won't count as a new partner, as gynecologists say.
    Any new partners? they ask, with that casual lilt.
    God no, of course not. I stick with historic deadbeats.

Despite the ions spinning up there, singing siren songs.

There's the man who hated real human females and decided to manufacture his own. He prepared drawings on architect's trace and molded three models the size of a Barbie until he had her right. Then he sculpted and rubbed and polished his dream, a life-size, candle-cool girl. Smooth, of course. Dream girls are smooth. Hair other than cascading from the top of her head? God, no, not on a dream girl.

Lucky that at Publix you can buy kits for home waxing, although more hands plus a mirror on the floor would help. I can't afford both waxing and highlights, and highlights I can't do myself. It hurts, waxing, either way, but at least this way it's cheap.

No swimming for a day to let the rashes subside.

It's only the Devil. What harm in that?

Swift shopping at Macy's. Cheap new dress.

I WAS SITTING in a salon on the Beach, with tinsel all over my head, when a white BMW pulled up right outside the glass doors. A young woman swung in with tight jeans and high shoes and lively breasts and gold jingling from her ears and wrists, and she swept through the salon until she found the person she wanted, a woman having a keratin treatment, and got the keys or money she needed and swirled out again, leaving our chairs spinning.

What was that? I asked Richard, foil and paintbrush in his hands.

Oh, her, he said. She's nasty. I mean she's gorgeous but she's mean. She's one of the girls who does the boats.

The what?

You know, he said. You hire them to be on your boat. In a bikini and what all. You've seen them on the front of those yachts.

Just *be* on the boat? An ornament?

Or maybe more, he said and shrugged.

Cross between figurehead and hooker?

He didn't answer, but after a moment said, There was another girl like her who used to come in all the time—and come to think of it, just three weeks ago she was sitting right where you are now—and he looked at me in the mirror, his face very sunned and creased. She was getting her hair unruined, he said. She'd done so much awful stuff to it, I had to strip everything away and get right back to nothing and then, anyway. She was here getting done for a show that night—she didn't actually do the boats, she was a dancer or something at one of the clubs, but the same type as that one just now—and she left here gorgeous, although she was not a very nice person, I have to say. But the next morning she was found in a Dumpster.

What?

Maybe you saw the story.

No.

Mm-hmm. Burned up in a Dumpster.

We were silent as he wrapped strands of hair in foil. I looked at him in the mirror, smelled hot hair.

Burned? I said.

Mm-hmm. Someone threw her in and lit it, or maybe killed her first, not sure. I guess she made her boyfriend or whatever man mad, and he was one of those types. I forget the details. I think she was Russian, maybe Ukrainian. Who knows? Maybe he didn't even know her.

SIRENS SCREAMED everywhere on the way home, trucks raging red over Alton and Dade. Smoke tumbled into the sky.

New notice in the mail room: old board out, new board in.

Good riddance! said Lino in the elevator. Told you I'd get rid of them.

He smiled with overlarge, overwhite teeth, eyes pink and small, a rabbit's.

SEE THE FOLLOWING in blurred blue light, please, and please play it fast:

Devil takes a cab from the airport, sending curt message with thumbs as he rides. Devil gets in the building, gets in the door, has long arms and legs spidering around me at once, trips me down on the bed. Mirrored walls watch—all this in blue light. Drinks are drunk on the balcony, smoke sent in rings from his jaws to the sky. Cab is taken Beachward, scotch drunk by Devil, sunny magenta Camparis by me. Devil rarely meets my eyes, although when I catch his shady violet ones they are always looking and glance away fast. Punish him by making him come in by the Dumpsters. So N won't see, or Virgil. Ovid wouldn't like what he saw. Or at least what I remember, because this is what I do with the Devil: make sure I won't remember.

Bottles on the floor, twisted cloth, smoke.

Devil departs early as he talks on the phone, flush with the deal he's struck with the Heat. Striding past the girl-trees by the chlorine fountain, he flicks a cigarette at their bark.

I MIGHT NOT have mentioned that my walls are mirrors.

Apartment came that way.

Showing you your bleak face no matter which way you turn.

Buster noses along the cold glass; patches of quicksilver are scratched away, black.

Also might not have mentioned the clock in the sky. Beyond Costa Brava and the Venetian, way over on the Beach, above the distant horizon of sea: a huge square of digital time.

Huge dancing light-girl west of the bay, and her mate, the huge clock to the east.

Beside the numbers, smoke keeps rising into the sky, a slow gray slanting tower.

Arson, maybe.

Maybe a girl.

*W*ELL, *THAT'S WHAT you get*, wrote K. *Doesn't mean you're ready to quit. That you even let him in is proof. Put on something nice and go sit in a bar and have a cocktail. So someone new with a pulse and a car will look at you, dammit, and remind you you're alive.*

COULDN'T STAND the apartment or Latin or poor Buster's howling anymore so went out. Walked not along the Venetian, but east.

As I crossed over the bridge, a yacht passed, beat booming around it. In the cabin, three men with drinks shouted over the music; on the prow lay two girls in bikinis. Both leaned on their elbows, toes pointed toward sea, long hair flitting, long legs bare, bare hips.

A posse of Jet Skiers roared by, musclemen in life jackets, engines roiling the surf. They whooped at the girls, bellowed pleasure and lust. The two sets of men, those on board and those on water, regarded each other, regarded the girls. Then all the men grinned and raised their glasses or fists to toast such splendid possessions.

The boat sped into a red ray of sun, and the girls on the prow: they flamed.

Walked north, away from the lounge chairs and plastic bottles jammed in the sand, walked north by thirty blocks. On the boardwalk: German family, two Latin ladies talking fast, skinny man selling crickets made of woven palm frond. Music thumped from hotels. But the farther north you walk the quieter it grows, until the boardwalk ends, and wooden steps take you to cool, pale sand.

A photo shoot. A guy was darting and pointing and shooting a young woman wearing only a thong. She rolled in the sand, rose to hands and knees, swung her hair and bare breasts and roared, then swiveled onto her back and scissored the sky, just a string of cloth between her tender inner world and everything else, broken bottles and jets and Dumpsters. Another woman danced behind the photographer and around him, finally pulled up her shirt, pulled it off, and flung herself on top of the other as her legs cut the sky. Three men had settled in solo spots fifty paces away, to watch. Two had their hands in their shorts.

Five blocks north lay something large at water's edge. From far away: beached dolphin? No: human, but not clear if male or female or what. It twisted, it wriggled; from the waist down, in frills of surf, swished back and forth a fish tail. Above the tail, a naked belly and thin, bare breasts, head flung back, eyes shut, red hair sweeping the sand. No camera to be seen. She stroked her belly with a ringed hand and looked so alone and private I wasn't sure whether to walk in the water and pass at her tail or walk behind her head. She didn't care. She swished her sequined tail in the froth, dragged her long red hair in the sand, held both breasts as she writhed, mascaraed eyes shut tight.

Someone is living on this beach.
  Wrote my heel in the sand, to the sky.

RAN INTO N on my way back in.

Look at your hair, she said. How *glamorous*. Do you have a date? *No.*

Well, it's only because you're too involved with that dead poet and those hopeless guys you write to. Plus all the men here are gay. I know it's a cliché, but it does reduce the possibilities. And I guess you don't want to try the inter . . . ? No, I guess not. Is it a sort of paralysis? No, I see. Maybe you're just not *interested*. Okay, well. Come up and have a drink with P and me. Not that it will help, but you know. Next Thursday. No, I see the hypnotist Thursday. Come Friday. You'll like P. I guess you will, anyway. I mean, *I* like him. But then, I did *marry* him. Anyway, he's younger than I am.

Nice change, I said.

But only by four years. Still, I'm the older woman. I had to teach him so many things, and she laughed the dry laugh. *Politics*, for instance, she said. It was the early seventies, and he was such a baby he didn't know anything. But I came from an old lefty Jewish family, I knew everything. And other matters. You can imagine.

Certainly can.

I'm only sorry—

About what?

Well, that he has to put up with me now. He wouldn't like me saying that. Poor P, he takes such good care of me. . . . He doesn't like me to do anything, not pay bills or clean or anything. When I used to be a nurse! I can't even be a real *wife* anymore. When he still seems so *young* to me, and vital! You know what I mean. Me being so broken and— She shook her hands and looked down at herself as if amazed that this was *her*.

What do you mean? And what hypnotist?

I didn't want to bore you with all of that. It's just . . . Oh, it's just I have so much pain.

Excruciating but invisible pain, she told me then, that began with running and yoga until her cartilage was worn away and she was just bones rubbing bones. Made worse by a surgeon who claimed he'd fixed her but hadn't. The pain was even worse after that, she said, although he said she imagined it. Nothing to do but believe her. Even if she walks erect and looks free as she floats in the pool: I believe her because she says it and because her eyes are always being abducted by something that seems to swim up from inside and wrench her back into hell.

But it's *okay*, she said. I'm working on it. Okay, so the therapist wasn't really that helpful, because you know *talking* doesn't do much. And the chiropractor was sort of a joke, but the massages can be good, and sometimes the acupuncture. For a bit. Don't get me started on herbalists. I can't believe I've become a person who does all this stuff. I never used to be this skinny. Look at me! But anyway, there's an energy therapist, that's where I'm going now. He's supposed to pull energy away from the pain or something. Also the hot tub can be helpful. And the pool . . . Well, the pool. We're lucky to live here, you know. It's paradise, right, she said, and shrugged, and bent herself into her car.

BONE TISSUE = CALCIUM PHOSPHATE + COLLAGEN. Makes bone rigid, like coral. Calcium phosphate is not organic, unlike calcium carbonate (of limestone, cement, and concrete), which is.

It's getting clear that I've been wrong about N and her husband, their being Want and Want Nothing. When she gets up, agitated, from a lounge chair and stalks over the cracked pool deck, her bone fingers clutching her riddled back, from beneath the brim of his baseball cap, her husband's eyes keep watch. They turn to his paper only when she looks back.

O N THE CAUSEWAY this evening, across the road from the silhouetted duck was a silhouetted iguana. Iguana gazing pensively south. Gazing north, the duck.

And suddenly I saw a painting in the dusky air: *An annunciation angel floats on one side of a column, a virgin sits amazed on the other. Between them, a beam of light.*
   I bring you a message from our lord! says the angel.

Messages, messages. Faraway men.
   Blue-ink letters from the other side of the world.
   Messages now are blue light.

Farther along, on Rivo Alto, a hen and five long-legged chicks jerked and clucked over the lawn of a palace, then rushed flapping across the street, making a Maserati swerve.

The sky just then: coral dunes.

Dancing light-girl on the west side of the bay; her mate, the huge clock on the east. The clock can be the angel here, delivering his message.
   Guess what, the angel clock's saying. *It's time.*

THREE

SMITH & WOLLENSKY: a fancy restaurant at the south tip of the Beach, with a bar out by the water that rushes through the Government Cut. Cruise ships pass on their way to sea, making the atmosphere festive. I perched on a stool, sipped a French 75, and spun around now and then to watch spangled chunks of city float by, miniature people waving. Bar-mates: two couples, a young trio, and a man on his own. I texted K that I was on a stool in public with waxed legs and candy-floss hair, solo man not distant. He ordered a rye and likewise cast his eye around, a glance that flicked on me, but passed; he focused on his rye and phone. Maybe Latin, maybe Anglo, but mostly not one of the deadbeats I know and thus *cento per cento* implausible.

Imagine an alien face drawing near.

I don't know how people do it.

When I was fifteen, the idea of a boy's face coming so close that it would dissolve in my vision made me panic. Like Zeno's arrow: for another body to get that close, it must not only blur but *melt* into me, and this was so paralyzing I'd laugh and bolt.

Was thinking this as I pondered the cheekbones of the Smith & Wollensky man. They glowed from his cell, and occasionally he smiled at the glow, looked up as if the phone-person were there, then shuttered again, dropped screenward.

Sipped and turned slowly around and around on the stool. After a while I wiggled off and walked to where the coral-rock path meets boulders that hold back the rushing water, and stared at ugly Fisher Island, and out to the black, black sea.

That's once, wrote K.

. . .

Two days later. Will do it three times because three points confirm a line. This time, an Italian restaurant and sports bar up the Beach. The owner, I've noted in reconnoitering, is tall and slim and has the face of a panther and a lustrous gray-black mane. As I walked in tonight he was speaking closely with a high-hoofed girl, twenty to his fifty, beneath a frangipani tree.

Frangipanis are so nice. They bear flowers before leaves: five smooth petals of coral or lemon pinwheel from branches that look like burnt bones.

Walked through the table-set garden, lights strung between branches as they'd been strung along the decks of the cruise ships, and took a seat at the bar inside, a U-shaped bar made of something like Bakelite, smooth and cool, soft greens and reds from a Latin sports station glowing on its surface, how nice to lay your cheek down and sleep. The bartender, I'd noticed earlier, rode a motorcycle with another woman stuck to her back. Low jeans, tough-boy T-shirt, slick dark hair, rough voice.

Dimmi, she said.

Ordered a truffle pizza and prosecco, leaned back, crossed slippery legs. A woman sat two stools down, her hair highlighted and cotton-candied like mine, skin damp on her upper lip.

She grinned at me, crooked. Howdy, she said. I've been here since five—and her foot skidded off the stool rung.

That's a good long time, I said. Having fun?

Oh, she said, oh, if you'd been here at six, was it six? Maybe six. A soccer team was here. Italian. Don't know why they were here but I have never, ever, seen such men. I'm hoping they'll come back. Do you think?

She swung her head toward the door, clutching the edge of the bar for balance. Just checking! she said, her face reeling back my way.

Not yet, I guess, I said, and looked at her pale pink fingernails and the smudged gloss on her lip.

But really, she said in a lower voice, really I just come for him—and she nodded toward the panther.

Yeah?

Oh, absolutely, she said. I'm here every day. Every night. And I know, she said in the same low tone, that he's got a thing for me.

At that moment he was consulting with one of the cooks, knuckles on his square linen hips. The high-hoofed girl sat outside at a table, staring at her cell, lovely olive face aglow, black hair a glossy stroke. The panther went gliding out with a glass he placed before her.

He does? I asked my bar-mate.

Well, yeah! she said. He always gives me special drinks and a discount on whatever I eat. Wait. Have I eaten? No—I mean, have I ordered anything? Giovanna!—she waved her pink nails at the bartender. Am I eating?

Of course you are, M. We always make sure you eat.

See? said M, and bobbed her head.

My pizza came, and M's tagliolini, and she told me she worked at the convention center and came here because she was sick of the other places on the Beach and besides: the owner. At some point a man came in, a conventioneer, and stood between the garden and bar, looking unsure where to sit. The panther glided over to him, glanced at the room, then smiled and led him to the bar and placed him between M and me.

I knife-and-forked my pizza and sipped prosecco, neck stiff because now I couldn't face M and had to stare straight ahead. Big screens silently showed young men in red, green, and white running. In the garden, the panther sat with his girl, long fingers stroking the table. At the next table, beneath the lights strung from slim Manila palms, a plump older man with a cigar leaned back and eyed three young women in short dresses sipping red drinks. Between his table and theirs, among the philodendra and citronella candles, a small furred face appeared.

I leaned forward: not a rat—too big. Not rabbit or raccoon, something cartoonish about it. Eyes too large for the face, and face too large for the body, which was the size of a puppy and ended in thin tail. The creature nudged between philodendron leaves, nudged near a woman's pearl-toned heel, came close to having its ear ashed by cigar. Foreign rat? Imported with bananas from Ecuador? A big boot landed near it just then, and it slipped back into the leaves. When I turned to the bar, the conventioneer was leaning close to M, who whooped and skidded half off her stool, but he caught her elbow; her nails set themselves in his sleeve.

She noticed me over his shoulder and said, Wait—hi! Weren't you here earlier? When the soccer team was here?

He snapped his eyes toward me.

I'm heading out, I said around his shoulder. Want to walk?

Oh no no no! she cried. I just got here! Didn't I?

Way too soon to go, the guy said, and gave me his back.

Paid and left.

And walking home in the sulfurous light, I realized: baby possum.

The third outing was last night. This has taken almost a week. This time, a place closer to home: over by Publix, across from the marina with aisles of restless shark boats, their internal red lights blinking. There was the old faux New York restaurant and the new Corsican place—chose New York. Cold and loud inside. Walked up to the bar. Boiled eggs sat inside a big jar; I slipped one out and ate it. Ordered fish and wine and swiveled to face the situation. Two men, each alone. No. A woman appeared—one of Lino's Russian light-girls! Neither she nor her man spoke. She pointed to the menu, and soon a plate of raw meat arrived. She pulled at it in tendrils with her fingers while he studied his cell.

The other man also looked at his phone. Then suddenly palmed it over and stared dead at me. And bark ran over my skin.

Sono chiuso! I wrote K beneath a street lamp. *All done.*

Nope, she wrote, *you'd rather bury yourself alive with those deadbeats and your dead poet and that dying old cat. It's a kind of emotional anorexia—*

Switched off the phone.

The moon was full, tide high, salt water slopping the seawall of Belle Isle. From the manhole bubbled foam. Airy pale damp puffs rose through the grate, hovered in a tender, jiggling mass, then drifted free and blew along the curb, flitted and skittered over the road.

Sea foam. Sea girls once, who traded tails and tongues, in love, for legs that felt like knives.

READ TONIGHT THAT a college girl has disappeared. Cameras on shop fronts show her, tall and lovely, loping along in the dark, looking drunk or drugged. These days, sure, she's been drugged. What some boys like to do. Thin beauty loping along like a deer. A jewelry-store camera shows her amble past, then shows a man in an alcove see her. He waits a moment, looks around, follows. She lumbers into another camera's view, the man now close behind.

Think I'm lost, she texted a friend.

Then she shows up no more.

And now have read a long awful story: another college girl told a reporter she was raped. Drugged, yeah, and taken upstairs. But not drugged enough to forget what she saw. The faces of the seven above her in the dark, shining bottles in their hands.

Seven men, or boys, or dwarfs, or gods, or wolves, or uncles, whatever.

Turns out she imagined this story.

This story.

My friend S types me what he thinks: *Why wouldn't girls imagine rape. They're being raped the moment they're born.*

TEN MORE O STORIES of wanting and not wanting to transmute, and it's already July.

There's the story about the girl in love with her father who sneaks into his bed when he's drunk. But I'm saving this for nearly last.

There's the girl who tries to sleep with her brother.

And the one in love with another girl who can't figure out what to do.

The first gets what she wants, her father, then begs to be extinguished. The second does not get what she wants and weeps until she dissolves. The third turns into a boy, gets the girl, is happy ever after.

Between passages, I keep checking on news about the lost college girl. But nothing.

Back to O and then back for news, but there's never anything. Can't keep dwelling like this.

Have started researching options for the duck.

Muscovy ducks are considered exotic. If I call Animal Welfare, they'll euthanize.

Muscovy ducks are not pelicans, as the lady at Pelican Island observed, so no, they will not adopt her.

Two ornithologists at the University of Miami had no idea what to do. Ditto Florida International.

A Muscovy duck website recommended capturing the duck and taking it to a duck shelter.

A veterinarian specializing in exotic animals also suggested capturing the duck and taking it to a duck shelter.

Both website and vet said that to catch the duck, just grasp it by the neck.

There are no duck shelters within five hundred miles.

This Sunday, taped behind glass on the board in the mail room was a notice:

Due to a flood in the Men's Spa, it will be closed until further notice. We apologize for the inconvenience.

(Actually "inconvenience" wasn't spelled within miles of right, but I didn't have the heart to transcribe it.)

Then on Tuesday, taped in the same place:

This notice will serve as an announcement that the Men's Spa has reopened.

But then just today:

Due to a flood in the Men's Spa, it is closed until further notice. We apologize for the Icoveninance.

What's going on? I asked a woman in the elevator.

She regarded me. Then said, Things are happening.

(Had only pictured dirty men clogging pipes in disgusting ways.) Happening how?

Well, the new board is just like the old board, she said. Except for who gets the money.

For what?

She stared at me. The *pool.*

But I thought—

She shook her head.

So someone's—

We'd reached her floor. She nodded, put a finger to her lips, and slipped out.

TONIGHT HAD DATE with N and her husband. Just one flight up, so I took the stairs, which open to a balcony at each landing. Walked down the hall and through a door out to the curved concrete balcony. Designed this way for rescue from fire by helicopter? Don't know. But that stairway balcony is much closer to the bay than my own, so I stood out there to gaze at the shining water. Way down near our dock floated a long palm frond. Flange, not fin or tail. Went into the dim staircase, up, and out to the next landing. When I looked down at the bay again, the frond suddenly shot off.

Ran down the hall and when N opened, said, Shark!

What?

Quick.

But she had a bottle of wine in her hand and was drifting toward the kitchen, where from the shadow emerged the form of P.

A shark, I said. I just saw one.

I'm not surprised, he said, appearing from the kitchen—appearing, close up, *much* more than four years younger than N. *Pinguis*, healthsome, gray-gold hair, eyes like evening sky.

P, this is J, called N. I guess you've figured that out.

You're not surprised by a shark?

Of course not, he said and gave me a glass. Bay's full of them.

How do you know?

He shrugged. I've seen them.

Sure they were sharks?

Yes.

No, I said. Things look like them. Dolphins, tarpon . . .

He regarded me patiently. I will send you a photo.

N came out, and we clinked glasses and stepped out to the balcony, the bloom of moist air, distant cityscape, sky.

I've been worrying about that lost girl, I said.

It's awful, said N. Any news?

No news.

Which isn't good news, said P.

But you never know, N said.

That's true.

We sipped.

So what about the mysteries in the men's spa?

An awful lot goes on in that spa, said N.

But the flooding?

P shook his head. It's a funny old building. Lots of history and politics.

Someone would *flood*—

P smiled. Sure. Someone who isn't happy.

With the new board?

Could be.

Well, Lino, I said, you know Lino—

Everybody knows Lino, said N.

Lino says the guys in the old board are all in the mob.

Actually, P said, Lino's the one who's supposed to be in the mob.

Little Lino?

P crossed his arms and nodded.

Oh, they just say that, said N. People say so much junk.

P shrugged. Could be true. I believe it. Once upon a time, anyway. Or still. Who knows? He's a shrewd little guy. He did want a new board, after all. And got one.

We gazed at the skyline, the Venetians, the pool.

At least he doesn't want the pool destroyed, I said.

Think so?

What?

P laughed. Like I said. Lino and the mob. None of those guys gives a damn. Except for who gets the contract.

Oh, the pool, the pool, the *pool*, said N. It doesn't *matter*. I mean, it's just a stupid swimming pool.

I looked at her, but she was staring away. And like everyone, a liar. For her it is not just a swimming pool: when she's in it, she's free of that body. You can see.

Well, P said, it's a hell of a lot of money for people. Plus the jackhammering, all the trees hacked down—

Oh, I know, I know, said N. I'm being stupid and selfish.

I wouldn't go that far, P said quietly. Don't be so hard on yourself.

It's these drugs. They make me so . . . *stupid.*

After a moment P said, But speaking of our pool, did you know someone died in it once?

Really!

During Art Basel. He was floating there at dawn, fully dressed. In a tux. Or maybe I'm making that up. Everyone assumed it was some kind of art. No one even called the front desk.

Who was it?

P shook his head and looked at N. They both shrugged and said, That's Miami.

We drank and looked at the deepening sky, a point of light becoming Venus beside a brightening slice of moon.

Did he drown?

Not sure, P said. But he didn't jump, anyway, like people thought. Look at the distance from the building.

N got up just then for a new bottle, leaving a wet circle on the table.

We sipped our wine and watched the dancing light-girl appear in the dusk, and I thought of the girl who does the boats, and the one who went loping into the dark, and the one thrown into a Dumpster.

Drugs? I said.

Sure, probably.

Now, at home, am sitting on the balcony. In the gym across the way, that box of light high in the dark sky, the dark-haired girl is running. Tall and slim, she stares at the metamorphic blue clouds but looks like she sees nothing.

On a balcony beneath her, a man talks into a square of light, a red point of light in his hand drawing spirals.

Beyond them both, a white point of light swells in the sky. Then a second, behind it, and a third: the first glows large and swings west.

Above them all, starry Orion and his sword tilt over the sea.

And beneath the stars, the girl runs on and on in her box.

Even running, you can stay still.

Or staying still, you can run.

Trees in a breeze.

If you count the swaying of trunk and branches, the wind passing through leaves, how far does a tree travel through air?

Beneath my hand—sudden green glow.

Sorry, Devil. *Chiuso.*

But when I clicked, no Devil: on the screen was the *duck.* Sleek black feathers spotted white, delicate barnacles crowning her beak, her pink-ringed black eye baffled.

Hello, duck friend. We must do something! She is getting thin. Can you meet on Sunday?

Yes! I typed with eager thumbs. *I'll bring—*

Another glow.

Another picture. No message with this one, nothing but blue-green water, our bay. In the middle was a tiny slim shadow. I scrolled and zoomed until I found it: a hammerhead shark. So small in all that blue.

I zoomed as close as I could, then looked a long time at its weird scalloped head, its strangely delicate gills.

AT SOME POINT I have to ask myself: have I been wrong about how I view this situation? If I consider the evidence?

The history of single-celled wandering, I mean. The chronic inability to either merge or divide, to be with another or split into two, into more than just me.

As if the intimacy issues, as K says, would not even let a tiny homunculus in?

I am no country for men.

Not even a little baby.

Revirgining is beside the point.

I've been virgin all along.

A tree.

*F*IVE SIX SEVEN eight nine ten eleven twelve thirteen fourteen fifteen—

Rest on the pool's cracked lip, gasping, wet chin on slick wet arm.

And gaze down at light zigging through the transparent blue, down to the dissolving concrete.

—one two three four five six seven eight nine ten eleven—

Palm fronds glimmer and sweep the blue ion sky.

O<small>N MY WAY</small> to the duck rendezvous, wondered about the other duck person. The name on the messages seemed to be Xla. Female? Basque? Who cared about this duck? Someone who walked the causeway, looked around, wasn't sealed by earbuds. Possibly someone who cycled or drove, but this did not seem likely.

Good luck with Duck, darling! wrote my mother.

Okay, okay.

Xla and I had agreed to bring water, food, gloves, sheet, pet carrier. The hope was to lure her out with food and water, nab her, jam her into the carrier, and transport her to the Miami Beach golf course, to join a Muscovy flock.

Stultifyingly hot and bright, and you can't carry a parasol while catching a duck. Wore a big visor instead, making a halo of shade around my head that did one-ninth the job. Early July: sun highest overhead?

We'd decided on this awful hour because the duck seems denatured by the heat and spends the hottest hours in her shrub.

I got there first, saw the duck huddled in the sea grape. To wait for Xla, I climbed down to the rocks by the water into a thin slant of shade.

Voices. Climbed back up to a black-haired girl and sulky-looking boy in a red baseball cap.

Hello, she and I said. Okay, how shall we do it?

Once it's out eating, said the boy, we should surround it, and one of us should be holding the sheet, and we should slowly draw in close—

I think we should all three already be holding the sheet and corner her into the shrub, said the girl.

But then it'll just go deeper in the shrub.

But otherwise she'll bolt and go into the water, I said.

Or the street, said the girl.

It won't go into the street.

She might.

Listen, the boy said, I've told you how we should do it. You should listen to me. You never listen to me.

I do! cried the girl. It's just—

No, you don't, and you want my help, and I do not give a fuck about this duck, but I came here to help *you*, and now you won't listen.

Wandered away to see how the duck was doing. Even deeper in her shrub. She *was* thinner—and trembling. Climbed back down to the rocks by the water to wait the conflict out.

After a few minutes, the girl's face appeared.

Okay, she said.

Climbed back up.

So what do you want to do?

We'll put out water and food, and then when she's eating, he'll chase her from behind to where you and I are standing with the sheet ready to catch her.

Well, that sounded not likely. But who knew. We all walked away toward the causeway as if we were just casually leaving, and then I acted as though I were just coming to feed her like any ordinary day. I put down a dish of water and strewed Grape-Nuts in a line that would draw her away from the shrub. The three of us quietly got into our positions, not too close to the duck, and waited.

The "A" bus motored by. A moped.

She came out cautiously, gulped the water, and was nibbling at the Grape-Nuts when the boy charged from behind. She fluttered and flapped, galloped past the girl and me, dropped down to the water, paddled off.

The three of us stood on the verge and watched as she sailed away, past anchored yachts, a black-and-white blot in the distance.

Well, I said. She won't be back soon.

The boy shook his head and walked up to their car.

I guess that might be it, said Xla. He doesn't think—

I understand.

Yeah. He doesn't think we should spend our time on a duck.

Okay, I said. Will you still bring water?

Of course! she said as she scampered to the Mazda that was already revving.

Slick with sweat and burning, I staggered back over the bridge and past the Dumpster into the building, barely able to see.

Well, maybe Duck likes being where she is, said my mother. Maybe she doesn't want to leave.

Fine, I said savagely. Except that unless I feed her and bring her water, she'll die.

Have you thought that maybe you're keeping her there by feeding her? Maybe if you didn't, she'd go.

She can't! Her wing's clipped! She's stranded!

There was a pause. Then my mother said, Darling. Don't you think that perhaps you—

Yes, I said, yes, I know. I know this is not a real way to live. I know this. It's better to be involved with people than ducks. But right now, you know, I'm on a deadline, and there's not much *time*—

And I wrenched the conversation back to her blood pressure and whether she was doing her leg exercises and drinking enough water and eating anything other than grilled cheese, and soon she was sick of me, too.

FAR OUT AT sea are waterspouts. Wavering lines of gray that dance between sky and sea or suddenly lift from the sea, disappear into cloud, then dip again, grow thick and blurred and race over the ocean. When exactly a waterspout becomes a tornado I'm not sure: over land vs. sea? A few clicks and I'd know, but I'd rather sit here on the balmy balcony and type with eyes far away, watching waterspouts waver. The smudged corollary of heat lightning, maybe. Watery corollary of smoke?

Hurricane in German = *Orkan*. The word used to sound to me like something alive. They'd rage over the Schwarzwald, ripping up pines being grown to be paper: I'd watch through our wide glass wall.

Forgot to mention July Fourth. Fireworks clear up the coastline. From the balcony I could see only the reflections of fireworks across the bay in the windows of Costa Brava, but at least they gave the sound for the others far to the north that I could see but not hear. Single bright lights silently rising, slow cascades of sparkle falling, silent but then an invisible boom. Are fireworks still made of pulped books?

W HEN I PASSED by on my walk this evening, there of course was the *duck*, in silhouette, gazing at the bay.

She warbled and came wobbling toward me for Grape-Nuts, but I just walked right by. Did not even turn my head. Kegeled.

I did not, do not, want to be a weird lady involved only with a duck.

And cat.

I *don't*.

Was walking over the drawbridge as a motorboat glided below—like a 1967 Mercedes convertible skimming the milky green. The one I learned to drive on, my stepfather turning from the dunes and darkening sea to regard my hand on the knob, my blowing hair, tanned colt knees, eyes unblinking toward the road. With a flick of a finger he bid me take it to sixty-five, seventy, who gave a goddamn what the sign said, this was a *Mercedes*: only fools followed the rules.

His rare, narrow-eyed smile.

Squinted own guilty eyes so only they knew if they glowed.

In the butter-yellow boat below me: two men, shirtless with firm, bare arms resting on polished sideboards. Healthy *pinguis* look to their flesh. The setting sun made their skin emit light, and by now my kegeling had resulted in my own lower glow—because the Human Body does what it wants and stirs up trouble no matter *what* you think best, and these men with their smooth lit arms and trunked laps slung into low leather seats—I couldn't help it, I glided up onto the bridge's balustrade and with uncommon grace stepped off and floated, floated, gently down, and was caught by the man on the left. He looked surprised but then seemed glad, and said to his friend, Look what I caught. That one glanced over and grinned; he had on sunglasses even though it was dusk. He placed his free hand on my calf, as it seems that I was suspended between the two, my head on the thigh of the other, cheek against a growing plumpness inside his trunks. His fingers—how hadn't I noticed?—had casually begun undoing my top, and now there were my breasts in the warm blowing breeze, as we motored out to sea!

*F*OUND THAT MAN *with a boat you were hoping for in glam-land, now that you hate me again?*

The Devil.

Two, in fact! Just today.

Y EAH, WELL, what's wrong with fantasy. *Phantasia*. Born of visions. Even if Aristotle calls it a feeble sort of sensation. An active fantasy life is *good*, as K says. Self-pleasuring *does* ward off atrophy.

Although why atrophy should worry a tree, I don't know.

Atrophy, emotional anorexia, paralysis.

Solipsism?

Oh, for fuck's *sake*: one does what one can.

In the middle of the park today, when I was on my way back from Publix with pink umbrella and heavy bags of milk and cherries and litter and cat food, sweat trickling down my arms, N emerged from the shade of the banyan. She stepped into the sun and held up a long yellow hand to stop me, squinting into the blaze from beneath her white hat.

Let me ask you, she said. Do you still have desire?

Blinked the salt-sweat out of my eyes and told her that I did, yes, but only in the abstract, no longer tethered to anyone real because Sir Gold, alas, was only ideal. Added a few scientific points about the healthfulness of fantasy, satisfying the need for blood to rush through and plumpen lower tissues and explode, brain simultaneously exploding in stars, etc.

Okay, she said. If you still have desire, you're still viable. That's how it goes.

Like purring and eating, I said.

Sure, she said. Why not.

• • •

But as I passed the synchronized swimmers and the fountain chortling its chlorine bloom, I decided she was wrong. Desire can't be desire if it doesn't slant out toward an object. That is a snake eating its tail.

Still, one does what one *can*.

*P*HANTASIA! HERE we go! Location, location, location!

When I was young the dream spot was always a green hillside at night, a golf course maybe, somewhere wide and dark and free, and I had an even softer brain then so made those hillsides Arcadia. Stretches of dark sloping lawn, perhaps a white pool of sand from which a hunter would rise. Alone, the two of us, in all that cool green, night sky above us full of pinwheeling stars, some of them once Ovid's girls who winked down to tell me I wasn't alone.

When I was older, the location became bars, dark and nasty and underground, me sitting on a stool as one man spoke to my face to distract me while another from behind undid buttons and zippers as I pretended not to notice, as my shy breasts appeared in the air, men's wet lips sliding all over them. Other men watching, always, a thicket of eyes.

It troubles me to have self-exploitive fantasies.

But not much.

These days I prowl around choosing new locations. They include the green verge where the bad men fish, a place where you can be made to lean over a rock and have all kinds of things done unto you. Or that big banyan in the oval park, that huge tree whose roots drop to the ground and form a dusky forest, with many dark bullish trunks you could be made to lean back upon. Also, the cave beneath the white spiral steps: always twilight down there. You could just pause after an evening walk and venture in there to find—

Most often, it's the red boat with chrome. Dancing and slinking, champagne bubbles, bobbing on the dark sea.

In the innocent mornings I walk in my bikini, with towel draped over head if the sun broils, and look at the boats, into the boats, into that small red paradise boat. And blush to think of what I'd imagined there the torrid night before, alone beneath the popcorn ceiling, as Buster cried and paced the mirrored walls.

Was walking farther on the causeway than usual the other evening, beyond Rivo Alto, beyond Di Lido, past San Marino, all the way to the next island whose name I can never remember, when I looked across the road where a black truck had parked, and a man in a wet suit stepped out from behind. He glanced my way, grinned, and disappeared into the ground.

I had to wait until five cars and a moped had passed until I could hurry across the street to see.

Mirage? Stepped from a dock just beyond, in fact, and not from behind a truck?

Nope.

Into a manhole.

Man. Hole.

So then that man, grinning before stepping into the ground; and the wet-suited one beneath *Paradise Found*, who looked up through the black brow of mask; and that one who rowed a surfboard, one I still think about nights alone—they've all become a single man. In my mind. Whether he lives in water or sea caves or a boat in the bay, I don't care.

There's nothing wrong with any of this.

Given that I'm capable of nothing real. Just a deadline for a dead poet, an old cat in diapers, a duck. And a mother not ready for Sunset.

Sunrise.

Use it or lose it!

A gynecologist's voice. Although just now can't remember whether the gynecologist said this to my mother, or me.

Ran INTO GOOD OLD Par-T-Boy today while walking on Di Lido. Was passing his house as fast as I could, and just then he emerged from the vegetal wrack. He stood among the broken tiles, beside a tilting hedge, and looked at me with comic outrage, hands in the air.

You walk by my house, he said, but don't knock on the door?

(Am translating his language here.)

Well, sorry, I said, but I'm walking. Walking is exercise, not stopping to chat. You'd want to chat.

Why would I want to chat? I don't want to chat. I'll walk with you.

(Oh, no: he waddles.)

But you like to pause, I said. No exercise that way. Nope. Sorry. Going.

Okay, okay, he said. Such a hard-ass. Let's go kayaking later, then.

(His kayak is mildew-slick and missing a seat and cracked along a side. He hides it beneath a neighbor's banyan, unknown to the neighbor, a fancy neighbor with frontage. To get to the kayak you have to scurry from palm to palm alongside the palace and hope the twin giant poodles who grow hysterical near humans are napping deep inside.)

Par-T-Boy was sliding a sprig of hair up his forehead. Am a man with a boat, y'know, he said. Thought that was what you wanted, now that you struck out with your dream boy. We'll sail around the Venetians. I'll pick you up at eight.

Exactly what I deserve, with the fantasies I've been having.

. . .

So now an afternoon of dread: impossible to focus on O. Went out on the balcony every half hour to check the sky for rain. Glowering, purple-blue in the distance, but no definitive rain. At five before eight gathered supplies, descended in the mirrored box, trudged through the paradise jungle, and spiraled down the steps to await Par-T-Boy on the dock.

After a time a small form emerged in the thickening light across the bay by Rivo Alto. It paused, and an oar shook at the sky, but when a motorboat thundered by I could see him weebling in its wake. Sat on the dock and shed sandals. The tide was rising—water sloshed at my toes—that sea current rushing through the bay, the anchored boats swiveling toward the sinking sun.

Then there he was, wobbling toward me in a slim plastic-shelled puddle, wrappers and bottles floating around his feet.

No little bench to sit on?

He waved at this preposterousness. You don't need a bench, he said. Sit Indian-style on the bottom.

Not wearing a bathing suit.

So what? he said. It's water.

What?

Come *on*, he said, so I gripped the boards of the dock and flopped into the dirty puddle.

I have done little kayaking and none with half an oar, and I couldn't tell if he was doing his part perched behind me on the bench, because we kept lurching one way, lurching the other, spinning around, and the seawater was suddenly so *dark* and slapping, and from the middle of the bay it was odd how far away Belle Isle looked as we rounded it, and I kept thinking, single scull, single skull, going all wrong in this single skull, but once we'd finally slashed our way to the middle current and were winging along in it, careening right toward the big iron drawbridge and then whooshing below it to circle the island, the purple sky I'd forgotten about suddenly exploded and waves reared up, the boat skittered down and up slopes, and the current hurtled us toward the Standard just as zags of lightning crashed through the sky, and at the Standard a party throbbed underneath awnings, bikini girls undulating in strobing lights, a gala Par-T-Boy wanted to attend but somehow he was not on the guest list, and so he'd concocted a stealthy entry, not via street but by water, and with luck a wave did slop us right at the wooden dock, I caught the edge of it just before we went tunneling under, and once I'd muscled us back and clear I climbed out, blistered, weak-kneed, and streaming, with a pink wrapper of something glued to my calf, as Par-T-Boy waved to a Manolo girl and flung an arm toward his bark to indicate the dangers he'd gone through to reach her, and I thought all *right* already and shouldered my soggy bag of supplies and squelched back safe across the road to Nine Island.

GOT HOME TO LEARN the college girl has been found. P was right.

In Ovid, this girl would have become a bear, or maybe, if lucky, a star. That's if she'd been taken and ruined, but then been shown rare mercy. But if, in Ovid, she'd instead managed to get away—if, once her hunter had shoved into his car her long legs and arms and slender central portion with its inviting passages; once he'd dragged her out of the car again and into a field to jam every part of himself into her as well as whatever came to hand, bottle, flashlight, gun; if, when he began to do all of this, to throw her onto the ground and begin his blissful pounding, she'd managed to scream into her legs to run, run, fucking *run*, and this girl was strong and fast and could *really* run, she had been faster than this big man and gotten free—maybe, in Ovid, she'd now be a tree or stream or airy wind.

Not what happened. He got her, got what he wanted. Doesn't take long. And this girl is no tree, star, or rush of wind. He just left her out there when he was done. She's a tumble of bones in a streambed.

NOT SURE I'VE really mentioned coral rock.

The most beautiful thing in Miami.

A limestone of fossilized reef that, when cut, shows in patterned section the different petrified corals. Elkhorn, staghorn, sea fan, starlet, labyrinthine-brain.

DOES IT SEEM fair to you that there's such a difference between the words "misanthropy" and "misogyny"?

How about "anthropologist" vs. "gynecologist"?

AND THERE'S THE story of the underground man who climbs from a hole in the earth and crouches low in the grass until he sees a girl, a girl in a field who's stalking a rabbit. He runs at her hard and pounces, holds her tight around the ribs, carries her off as she kicks and bites. Or let's forget the rabbit and have her gathering shells instead. Or maybe she's picking up trash on the beach, bottle caps and shreds of plastic bags and, gingerly with a stick, used condoms. Maybe she feels an affinity with trash, scraps of material everyone thinks are worthless, when really nothing is worthless, she knows this, everything was worth something once, everything should be cared for and saved. Anyway. He bursts out of his hole in the sand like an enormous malignant crab and clutches her and carries her off, and along the way something of hers gets ripped and falls, maybe an earring or bikini bottom, yes, it's her striped bikini bottom, and that piece of dirty cloth lies on the sand once he's dragged her underground, the only sign she'd ever been.

YESTERDAY TWO people sent messages about the duck, but not helpful.

Contact Animal Welfare!

Take it to Pelican Island!

Now that I am the duck's sole tender, saving her is up to me. I elevatored down to the leaking garage and got in the Mini, drove over the Venetian, dollar twenty-five toll and all, ramped onto I-95, and sped along in the white-hot light until 95 dumped me onto Route 1. Then way down Route 1, which ought to run beneath the Metrorail for shade but doesn't, to a sporting goods store. Went in and told the man there I needed a net. He was tall with damp-looking bristle on his face.

Fishing? he said.

No. A duck.

He didn't exactly smack his chops but looked eager and asked how much the duck weighed.

Eight pounds? No. More like a big chicken, maybe six.

He stared at me, eyebrows riding his forehead.

A six-pound duck? he said. Can't you just grab it?

She bites and is quick, I said. It's hard.

I won't transcribe the rest of the negotiations, but thirty-two dollars later I had a net fixed to a pole. Was excited to try it out—would need Buster's carrier nearby but not noticeable to the duck, and then stow her in the car.

But as I drove home, the blue sky exploded again, as it does every afternoon these days, so no attempts to capture duck.

When I got back to the Love Boat, three plumbers' vans blocked the way to the garage. And in the mail room, taped to the board behind glass:

Due to a flood in the 5 line of apartments, water will be shut off for that line tomorrow from 9:00 until 2:00. We apologize for any inconvenience.

Then, this morning, when I went down to swim:

Due to a flood in the 11 line of apartments, water will be shut off for that line tomorrow from 9:00 until 2:00. We apologize for the inconvenience.

Paced up and down the dock postswimming, with towel draped over head, glancing into the boats and water, but otherwise pondering condominium crime.

What's with all this flooding? I asked the Frenchman in the elevator going up.

He raised his eyebrows. Don't you know? He grinned and said, It's *sabotage*. Some people are not happy with decisions by the board.

The old board is flooding the new board's apartments? How do they even get in?

Ha ha! he said. No problem. Not in a building like this. Everyone is rotten. Everyone has a connection. It's all about *concrete*. And—

He made the money sign with his fingers as we walked down the vegetal hallway, then opened his door to a flood of barks.

My apartment door opens to a flood, too, of howls. When Buster's travels are blocked by a table or chair, he plops to a skinny hip and yowls. I don't think he hurts. I'm sure he doesn't hurt. I think he just can't hear himself—like the Human Body on the causeway, panting loud with earbuds in. I don't know. So I pick him up, which startles him, and hold him and rock with him on the black leather sofa, until he purrs and his claws sink into my skin.

At least the diapers have helped the other issue, because with this swirling cork floor it can be hard to identify liquids et cetera, and I was getting worn out by all the wiping and mopping. The diapers mostly hold, but he overflows sometimes, limping around with a heavy sog between his skinny black-and-white haunches, snail-line of wet behind him.

But it's still not time. I know it's not time. It can't be, because he purrs.

Flooding everywhere! Not just the men's spa and those lines of apartments and that watering woman upstairs, but the sky, the ground: so much traffic between sky and earth and sea down here. Lightning, fireworks, waterspouts, jets. It rains every day at four o'clock. If you're sitting on the balcony you can watch the rain come—it can be a pleasure watching the rain come, just sitting still and letting the world go. To the west, over the causeway and beyond the bay, where sandbars emerge at low tide and motorboats scallop the water, above all that, the sky is slowly overtaken by scuds of deep soft gray. First those thick gray banks roll over the horizon, then they draw so near they dissolve into skeins of water that hide the city bit by bit, a moving dissolution. You can watch the streetshine creep this way, slowly blurring buildings and parks, a zone of shine moving down Dade, over the bridge, and down the causeway, and exactly then you smell rain on hot pavement. As soon as you do there's a hitch in the air and you'd better run inside fast because all at once spray is whipping your windows and you can't even see Costa Brava. The rain slashes at a slant, streaming across the glass. Inside I sit and hold Buster, watching rain river down the windows, the hurricane doors rattling in their tracks.

. . .

Well, it is the season, said N.

I'd run into her and P waiting in the garage, all of us having hoped to escape, to go out for a walk after one long downpour looked about done, but no, another explosion. Water spewed up from the garage's drain holes, spewed up hip-high and thunderous. Outside, through the garage grate, water gushed from manholes and storm drains along the pink sidewalks, foaming, frothing, rivering over the curbs.

Hurricane season, I mean, said N, and when she did I could see the radar line clocking, searching for the telltale eye.

P gripped the garage's grate and half-hung, gazing out at the pour. The whole city will be underwater in thirty years, he said. Or sooner! To say nothing of this derelict place. He lifted his hands from the grate and laughed.

Funny man, that P: a glaze of jolliness bright over despair in his eyes.

Suddenly the roaring slackened, then stopped, and through the grate came blaze and steam. On the sidewalk lay bright pools of sky.

Thank god, said N. Let's go.

She pushed the button, the grate rose, and she and P passed into sunlight. But I waited and looked up at the giant belly of the pool, hanging down in the dimness, surrounded by cars.

Now that it was quiet, could hear a steady patter of dripping water. Water rich with chemicals and time slid down the pool's stalactites, making dark glinting puddles on the garage floor. And the belly of the pool itself: its rough concrete hide was like an ancient cave. You could almost see upon it the painted antelopes and aurochs, the dead man lying on his back, and beside him, the bird and the spear.

I TOLD MY mother that I knew being alone was not a real way to live. Like everyone, though, a liar. *Doch, doch.* It's the realest way. If you tend to a blind cat and stranded duck, and fragments of men drop into your in-box, and you talk now and then to a skeletal lady and wobbling old mother, and text occasionally with people your age, and focus on bringing a dead poet to life, surely that's enough.

Snow White had seven dwarfs, after all.

Must have added up to something.

I mean it. If a person drives herself around and has her own place and can fix most things or find and pay someone who can if she can't and is able to dig up inner resources to sustain herself even in bone-dry moments, absolutely baked and bone-dry moments, and if she has long since decided that for fuck's sake it's all right to drink alone—I mean, come on, there's no one to drink with—and if she's also decided that self-pleasuring is more than fine, it's health-some, especially if accompanied by fantasies drawn from excursions into the world: that's fine.

I tried this out on N today and got her slow sad smile.

It's good for a person to have another person, she said. It's good to have a mate.

LINO WAS IN the elevator this evening when I was going out for my Venetian walk, wearing the usual FitFlops and the same shorts I wear every day and have probably worn for three decades. Lino looked me up and down. Beside him stood a brontosaurus in white sneakers, white shorts, white T-shirt, blue belt, with thick, brass-bright arms and legs.

You a personal trainer, too? said Lino.

Me? No. Just a civilian resident.

Lino peered at me from under his hat, this one white straw with a pink band. Okay, I might have seen you here before, he said. Maybe. He hooked a thumb at the man beside him. This is my personal trainer, he said. Say hello to the lady.

The trainer grinned a gold-toothed grin and said something that sounded like *Chiello*.

(Russian? Bodyguard? *Hit man*? They actually exist and will come to old Love Boats? A guy to bust in and flood apartments and spas?)

You're helping Lino get fit? I asked.

Ha! said Lino as the doors slid open. He'll do more than that!

Oh?

The bodyguard smiled at his sneakers.

ANOTHER ETIOLOGY. Aristophanes' spheres in Plato's story (the spheres everyone seems to be writing about these days, even though *I* have loved them privately for decades and even wrote them into my marriage so-called vows): Aristophanes' spheres, the happy monsters that were each made of two people, man-woman or man-man or woman-woman, rolling around with four legs and four arms and two heads and hearts each, private parts squashed together. The only way to be whole was to be two. But these compounds were too strong, and a lightning bolt split them apart. Now they, we, spend our lives looking for our lost other halves.

No.

No other halves.

This is what I thought as I swam fierce laps, gasped at the lip of the pool, my legs swaying away each time I entered Fran's gyre, the unstoppable gyre of the senior club I am joining, and stared up at twenty-four stories of balconies, cloaked in the Love Boat's long shadow that each day leaves a little bit sooner.

Come closer, closer.

As Sir Gold once whispered to me.

W AS WALKING toward the drawbridge along the green verge when a Jet Skier skimmed extremely loud and close, so close he almost ground into the rocks and I could see the sleekness of his skin. He was in black, his Jet Ski was black, and I stopped and looked at his forearms, his strong hands on the horns of his machine.

Then I just stepped gracefully off the bridge and skimmed down, down, slipped behind him, my legs clasping his wet legs, my breasts pressing his taurine back.

Let's go, let's go, let's go to the sea!

Standing up there with bony elbows on the dirty concrete, old feet in cracking FitFlops, as below me he whipped and spun in the water and froth, delighting like a dolphin.

Out of the blue I thought: *Look at me!*

Now!

He rode on. He drew a huge spraying circle in the green, looped into another circle, digging, churning, cutting deep, dredging and ripping, spraying water and fuel-stink and engine screech, bucking and plowing, all horsepower, manpower.

Something cold stirred within me. I thought: *Harm should come to you.*

Then forgot about him and walked on past the duck, first island, second, past the old pear-shaped man who goes around with a bag to feed the cats, the old man I am becoming, past the crazy boy who swoops on his banana bike, although he's way too big and fat for it; he always shouts Hello, I always shout Hello back; past the HAREM-car house, smoking inside with sinister sex, could see it in the fogged glass. Then, walking back, there was the sunset, splendid as always, and a person gets tired of appreciating the damned sunset, having to keep stopping and turning to look at it more, with tourists on the Duck Tour–mobile taking sunset selfies.

Enough with the sunset.

Like everyone, a liar. I *do* appreciate it! Beauty like that—makes you helpless. Makes me walk home stupidly backward, filling eyes with color.

At the Love Boat, walked as usual past the Dumpsters and through the gate over the soft grass by the mahogany tree. Skidded off FitFlops and lingered on the tender silky blades, then walked along the dock, peering into the water because, you know, that's living the life.

From the dock, something ahead of me suddenly slid into the bay. Not the first time this had happened: I once startled an iguana sunning on the dock and it slithered fast and plopped in; by the time I reached the spot, it had become a fish. There this thing was now, in the water plugging along with a beak and clawed wings batting. I crouched, crawled sideways as it platypussed along. Feathers? Fur? Webbed feet?

Meanwhile became faintly aware of a sound—the kind you hear without properly hearing, whatever the phrase for such ephemeral sensory experience is. Maybe boys shouting on Monument Island, maybe someone singing on a boat, nothing you'd lift your head for.

So didn't. Kept peering into the water trying to decipher the bird, lizard, or fish.

But then the noise began to lift from the air, to clarify itself in my ear. It was a voice. A man's voice. A man's voice shouting *Help*.

Stood and scanned the bay, darkening, the sun nearly sunk.

Tiny and distant: *Help!*

In the bay's swift middle river, a coconut rolled. Far away by the verge, a Jet Ski bucked alone.

But no voice would rise from my throat.

Stone, a tree. Could not speak or move.

But as I stood frozen, from above:

Hold on! I've called! They're coming!

I finally jerked to life, ran down the dock, spiraled up to the pool, through the jungle and the glass doors, into the mezzanine, down the hall to Virgil, who was already running with his walkie-talkie.

I followed him back out, and we watched from the dock as a police boat whizzed under the drawbridge, then slowed, circled, and stilled, and a small man was pulled from the bay.

Lucky guy, said Virgil. Lucky somebody saw.

Rose to my twenty-first floor, not catching own guilty eye in the mirror. Then opened my door to see just the end of it: Buster spinning, nails scraping crazily at the floor, as if being lanced by lightning. Liquid flew from him—he'd flown right out of his diaper—his wild paws slid and he skidded and slipped, but clambered up because he had to keep spinning.

There's nothing you can do. Just wait until it's over, steer him gently from corners and table legs that could hurt.

Spinning, the sound of his panting, the clicking of nails on the cork.

Oh, baby cat.

Finally the lightning was spent and he collapsed, puddled black on the floor. I lifted him and held him close and warm in a towel, his little head slumped on my arm.

They don't know where they are after a seizure, the vet says. Even if they're not blind and deaf, too. Important to hold him awhile.

Sat on the sofa and stroked the wet fur between his long ears, down his knobby back, in his little underarms until he slept. Then put fresh tissue in his box and laid him gently down.

My mother's voice on the phone was soft.

Don't you think, darling, she said, don't you think all of this might be telling you something? Maybe—something might need to change.

W ELL, IT WAS a long time, in Germany. You can't help but start to feel it: hundred percent an alien. Ten years there, five years staring out the greasy train window at dawn on my way to the *Frauenklinik*. Then the greasy train window home again hours later, the greasy window of the tram, and back to our bare apartment sixty-six concrete steps in the sky. Then the wall of windows looking out at the gray, when I'd come in with a fresh bag of vials and needles, to start a new month of trying.

Calendars kept count. First the calendar with a polar bear, lorikeet, pink-bottomed monkey; then the calendar with a ghost gum, baobab, poinciana; then the one with types of rock. I like metamorphic rock most, but you'd probably figure that.

Dry German sun came in the window, on days when there was sun. Otherwise lead air, lead sky, wet weighty cloud. Same ads each season at the tram stops, year after year for ten years, same glares from old men, old women, cigarette smoke in the sooty air, broken bottles, puddles of piss and beer and rain.

Schöne Schlitz, a drunk once said, pointing between my legs. My husband didn't notice, maybe dreaming something else, but anyway, did nothing.

Schöne Schlitz, sure, I thought. Schlitz good for nothing.

In the summer, wisteria grew inconceivably huge from a small pot on the ground out front. It rose lush and weighty all the way to our floor and hung so thick across the wall of glass that it made our place a terrarium, green light. I'd hang little mesh bags of suet and seed in the leaves, bags I bought at Schlecker. Hung four across the wide glass, and sometimes two or even three little bandit birds would peck at a time, as I sat at the white table inside and watched.

A pair nested in the leaves each year, those little bandit birds. Two eggs, sometimes three. Watched until they cracked and opened, noisy skinny chicks, and flew.

Buster watched the birds, also. Year after year.

And watched me, too, ears alert when I'd sit on the bed again, crying.

Down on the street, seen through a hole I'd cut in the leaves, my husband would sit at the tram stop. Sit on the dirty bench with his satchel, holding his face in his hands.

Maybe tomorrow, maybe someday, as the song says.

Finally, when there was just nothing left, I split up our things and flew over the ocean. Stayed a time with my mother.

Then, the hopeful tour of old boyfriends. Lurch, Mick, the Devil.

Then that month with Sir Gold.

And then, now.

IN THE SKY this evening, as the sun set, as colors arced from shale far at sea, up to deep blue, then falling through sheer blue to pure glow to lime, coral, and rose, there was suddenly a radiance high in the clouds to the north: light struck clouds far higher than sunlit clouds can ever be. I leaned out on the balcony, looking. The glow intensified, became a small bright sun that rose and rose, trailing a thin darkness beneath it. In the park below, a man pointed up for his little girl to look, and both tilted back their heads. A boy on a scooter stopped, too, leaned on one leg to watch. And at Costa Brava, one of the runners stopped running and pressed against the chill glass to see: the shuttle's final launch.

We all watched as that small sun rose and then split in two, and half fell away, and the single flame rose and rose until it was gone in space.

AT LEAST I CAN still try to save the damned duck. It is so hot, nearly August, blistering scorching *shattering* hot, and from ten until six she huddles in the sea grape waiting for water, for the day to die. I see her there at midday when I can't stand being inside anymore and can't stand transmuting and looking for messages, so go outside in the flaming heat under my hot pink umbrella.

The duck *is* thinner; she trembles.

Enough. Today I am going out with the net. If she's weak and addled I'm more likely to catch her. I am determined to catch her. Will hydrate, put on the big visor, gather Grape-Nuts, water, and net, and head out to capture this duck.

—four five six seven eight nine ten eleven twelve—

No DUCK. THREE cars slowed down to watch me try. She waddled toward me as usual, thinking I bore only Grape-Nuts and water, then spotted the net and fluttered hysterically around, hopped down the rocks, sailed into the bay.

I stood roasting with my net. A car pulled over, hand out the window taking a photo. Outside the bridge house the bridge lady watched.

Am done. No more trying to save the duck. Just bring her food and water and let her live her stranded life.

When I got back to the Love Boat, two police cars idled out front. I went around to the trash containers to ask Tina what was happening.

She looked up from writing down the numbers of packages with her pungent black marker and said, Blood. On the wall.

Really!

She nodded, eyes stern. Things are getting ugly. I've been here twenty-five years and thought this building was as crazy as it could get, and now this.

But where?

The steam room.

Whose?

The men's.

No, whose blood?

She opened her eyes wide. No one's saying.

After stowing net in Mini, went dazzled out to the dock, picturing two eighty-year-old men slamming each other into the tiles, one breaking a fragile beaked nose. Or one of those stealthy playboys pummeling another one's head in rage, or someone else pummeling the playboy? But no, surely then there'd be an ambulance, too. Blood extracted some other way and smeared on the wall? The mirror? Inside the steam room, or the sauna? Was the men's spa just like the women's?

I hurried along the dock, up the spiral staircase, past the diving girl-tree, over the cracked concrete path, through mahoganies, bottle brush, slim Manila palms, past the pool to the spa rooms.

Virgil was standing at the door with his arms crossed and shook his head when I asked.

Bad things happening in there these days, he said.

Actually dangerous?

He looked down at me gravely and said, Yes.

All because of the pool?

A lot of money involved, he said. And you know people are wicked about money.

But, he said after a moment, rubbing his neck and squinting, it'll all be over soon.

HAVE WALKED OVER to the Beach, but this time went south. Past Flamingo Park, black-and-white balls being kicked on the grass beneath she-oaks, past neon balls being hit in clay that's often an inch of red liquid. Past the old buildings that old Fran helped save, the salmon or lemon Deco buildings now a-throb with the young in one another's arms. Over the sinuous pink sidewalk to the low dunes, the beach, the lines of lounge chairs that once were not there, and the plastic bottles left in the sand, waiting to join their friends at sea, pioneering a brave new island.

Men-of-war, too, are stranded on the crusty sand, their fabulous bodies not single islands but archipelagos: pink crests, blue balloons, long, virulent strands. Also moon jellies and regular jellyfish, too. In some places, they're all called medusas.

Okay, why not: Medusa. One of Ovid's girls whose name has lived on. She's another one raped! So many raped! Why are so many girls being raped! In this case, a girl whose greatest beauty was her hair (says O), which, like a glittering gold-sequin swimsuit, caught the bad attention of a monster of the deep. A god, again, or so you think, you're looking at him full of awe, so hard to believe that a god could be there, standing on the sand and studying you, so beautiful, you just can't believe it! And the world you've known until then might have been a bright thing, seashells and sky and water lapping your toes, and who knows what you might find in it: marvels. Then suddenly he smiles and steps toward you, does not care about the film of air you still need around you, pushes his hands right through it and throws you down. All the pounding, the salt, so hard to breathe, your skin ground into sand. Then he goes striding back where he came from, but you—everything around you turns to stone.

WELL, LOTS OF us have woken with everything wrong. Naked in a swimming pool, barefoot on an icy street. No panties, on a curb somewhere. Or in a grassy field, a field one might have loved that could have been Arcadia once, alone, back scratched, stinging bloody mess between legs.

"Regrettable sex." Is that what they call it now?

Yeah, well. Who told you to ride the shark?

HAVE DRIVEN TO the Everglades. Am in excursion mode. Over the MacArthur to I-95 and then west to the last road between so-called civilization and ruin. Then on until ruin gives way again to something good, long grass and runnels of water. Best things in the Everglades—aside from waving liquid grass and owls whose heads turn slowly, owls O knew well, owls always watching when things are bound to go wrong, crying warnings when girls in love with their fathers slur toward their fathers' beds—best things are tree snails whose tiny clean shells look painted, and solution holes.

Solution hole.

Where limestone's been cratered by acid in rain.

Solution hole.

An oxymoron?

Or maybe, instead, an answer?

Soluere = solve, dissolve.

When I came home, walked around back and saw P by himself on the dock. He lay on his back on the wood planks, late afternoon light slanting upon him. He'd rested one bare foot on a knee, his skin lit and lovely. He held binoculars and scanned the sky, scoping the deepening blue and tropical clouds. His bare toes clenched once or twice, his foot waggled—a little boy's delight.

WHEN ARE YOU coming? asked my mother on the phone. You're still coming, aren't you?

Of course!

One doesn't turn eighty every day, she said.

Exactly why I'm coming. Wouldn't miss it.

And what will we do?

We will have *fun*.

Two ladies, she said, on the town.

Across the way, at Costa Brava, on the corner balcony of the seventeenth floor, that young woman who has people come drum is sitting surrounded by paper. Origami paper, maybe, the colors of parrots, poincianas. She sits with one foot planted on the seat beside her, doing something I can't make out. She seems to be folding the edge of each sheet of paper, gluing one to another. Creating something that is starting to look large.

Floors above her, people still run. The tall girl and the boy who times his visits to the gym so he can run beside her, though he, like she, stares ahead through the wall of glass to the western sky.

Are they running together?

Are they really either of those words?

A PERSON, IN FACT, not only can live perfectly well alone but also does not need pleasure.

Other, maybe, than the sort she might get watching a rainstorm sheet through the sky, or going out on the town with her mother.

Or swimming.

Because there you are in the dark beneath the popcorn ceiling, wearing a silk nightie with straps that can be slipped off the shoulders as if by someone else's hands, silk that can feel marvelous when drawn slowly across small pink portions of flesh; there you are, ready, having looked forward to this moment of small pleasure after a day of Latin and changing diapers on a cat and feeding an impossible duck and getting no messages, nothing, from no one, not on your screen and not in a bottle, which does, yes, make you drink wine until you start to slur some over the oceanic cork floor in a mirrored box floating high in the sky, the spinning cold sky, and drinking alone is not a good idea, I *know*, but what the fuck when there's no one else there, which takes us back to the problem. So there you are, hankering for a small moment of pleasure of the sort you once had with a husband you really did love as well as you could and with a devil you should never have touched but he was hard to refuse, and of course with the *one*, the one who first split open your stupid young heart and you have never, ever, forgotten him, especially when he sailed back your way thirty years later and said Ahoy!, making you think that just maybe a miracle could happen and you would not remain the single-celled freak you seem to be, the paramecium or euglena you seem to be, something you so much don't want to be that you contrive fata morganas of rationales for why it's right to be alone, fata morganas that shimmer positively as you walk and walk alone on the Venetian but then when you are back in the musty old Love Boat, in this mirrored and corked box high in the sky, and have locked the door behind you, those fata morganas do what they do: dissolve into the stratosphere. Anyway. It's the end of a day, and there you are with the silky straps in the dark, and you shut your eyes and begin to play the fantasies that will help. Fantasies of the men you've been gathering to pretend there's something real here. Lying on the board of that tall stern man as he rows . . . Drifting down to the boys in the speedboat . . . Stealing at night aboard the small red boat and finding the wet-suited man, both surprised and waiting, and it's dark but with gleams of light coming off the water, and you stand as if fascinated by the glimmers through the gently rocking window, and he comes behind you and very slowly runs his hands all along your curved silken sides and then lifts the back of your nightie . . .

So there you are, you've constructed the scene, you've put together a hopeful conflation of men, you're picturing it all and trying to imagine that your cold dry hands belong to somebody else.

But then it's like a spout of water that is just too weak. The mind wanders, tries to focus, but wanders again, the hands lose interest, they fall still, the whole thing dies away. Nothing is stirred, nothing moves, nothing comes of this, nothing.

W ELL, THE TRANSFORMATIONS are logical. Ovid made that very clear. The transformations are fair. You become what you were bound to be; you become what you actually are. Wasn't it stone you wanted to be? Or glass, chrome? Something like that?

V IRGIL WAS RIGHT, too. After the floods in the steam room and those lines of apartments, after the blood on the men's spa wall, there came a final, invisible spasm. We knew what had happened by a notice in the mail room, with its bright hive of tiny brass doors.

Now that a Contracting Firm has been selected for the Pool Project, the pool and garden deck will be closed as of August 15. Until further notice.

How long do you think? I asked the Frenchman.

He laughed. They say two years, which means at least three. And the whole jungle garden will be cut down—he sliced with his hand and laughed—and the koi fish will die. The contractors will say not, but we know how they are. He shook his head. And for this we get to pay nine million dollars. Nine. Which means each of us must now find at least twenty thousand.

Lino walked by with a grin just then, tipping his blue-banded hat.

Yes, said the Frenchman once Lino had passed. Nine million dollars, all going to that little man and his friends.

Well, okay, said N. It's not the end of the world. Just a stupid swimming pool.

But oh, like everyone, a liar, that N who transforms in the water, where for a time she does not have that body and does not feel that pain, pain you can see lance her.

I swam in the hourglass this evening, the last time for a long while. Just glided through the cool with eyes shut. Bare arms and legs wide, floating, depth belling below.

I opened my eyes and looked up at the dusky sky: Venus hung bright by the moon. Then looked over to the building. Up on the twenty-second floor, out on N's balcony, stood P. He was leaning on his elbows, gazing down at the pool, and me.

I lifted a hand to wave. But he turned quickly away.

I WONDER. WAS IT ever anything other than two people running side by side, never getting closer?

For instance:

The Devil inside me the last time. Fucking and fucking, it wouldn't end, as if the point of fucking were maintaining a state of perpetual need whose satisfaction was its own continuation, pushing into me again and again until I'd gone from near pleasure to pain to numbness to rage, thinking, You are alone, all you want is the ongoing fucking. I pretended to sleep, to be dead, so he'd know I knew his fucking had nothing to do with me, and when he came out of his trance every now and then and said, Are you here? Are you here? Are you with me? I lay in a furious torpor, which didn't stop him, he kept right on fucking, his sick state of not-having and having at once.

Or:

Two people, husband and wife, on a bed. The light from the windows on the north is cool blue; from the south, through the wisteria, green. The parquet floor is laid on concrete, so all the sounds are hard. A new place where no one had yet lived when they carried their boxes up ten years before. Now, wisteria grows up to their fifth-floor wall of glass. A delicate spider dwells in the cold bathroom corner; the wife likes to observe its progress as she bathes. The black cat with long white whiskers and brows and a white spot on the nose is draped on an Ikea chair, glaucousness glazing one eye, for he is getting old, this once prancing boy-cat, fifteen years old. It's late on a Sunday, because again they have been avoiding this all weekend until now, when it is too late.

Can't speak of it any more than has already been spoken for four or five years. Spoken of by her, anyway; he can't bring himself to speak.

They have failed again, the two of them. They just can't love each other right. He weeps dry into his elbow, again; again, she stares at the ceiling. A feeling of hot bones in skin on a bed. Of something in your skin that *must* burst but can't: you are trapped inside. Four or five or six years of these Sundays, but who would count such a thing. This is after the years of careful calendars, the five years of animal, vegetable, mineral calendars, which kept track of temperatures, injections, and blood, until this pair was told on the phone that *es löhnt sich nicht*, was not worth their trying.

Outside, now, through the wisteria, down past the tram wires, on the gray street, the posters at the tram stop have shifted through their yearly cycle. Always the same poster each May; May is the time for the deodorant ad. *Unwiderstehlichen Achselhöhle!* Irresistible armpits. October would be the time for the bank poster. And no, she can't buy mesh bags of seed for the tiny bandit birds now, because it is May. In May you are not allowed to feed the birds. You may go to the drugstore, to DM or Schlecker, and ask *bitte* for the small mesh bags, but the ladies will shake their heads.

Nein. It is time for those birds to eat elsewhere.

FAR OUT IN the bay, a man swims from one boat to another. All you can see is a small splash of arms in the rippling green, near where that hammerhead swam. The distance between boats is maybe two blocks.

I will watch until he has reached the next boat.

A boy once tumbled from his father, out of blue sky, and splashed into green sea just like this.

Feathers, wax, sun.

Have I mentioned that O had a daughter? Or maybe she was a step-daughter: it didn't matter to him. He was teaching her to write stories, just before being exiled from Rome.

And when he was ordered to live and die alone on the Black Sea, she's one of the few he sent letters.

My dear darling girl.

I FORGOT TO mention what's in N and P's apartment that surprised me: among polished fossils and vases of plumes and ferns were candies. Chocolates, truffles, drops wrapped in scarlet or green or golden foil, as well as the brass molds to make them: stars and crescents, eggs and hearts, snowflakes, butterflies, fleur-de-lis.

What is this? I asked N.

It's P, she said. Haven't I said? His business. Making candy.

Making candy but not in Miami. Canada, in fact: he flies there each week.

Why? I asked him, in the garage. Why are you in Miami?

He shrugged, smiled weakly, and said, Oh, for N. I thought it might help.

BOUGHT A WEEK'S worth of diapers, pills, litter, and cat food, gave N instructions, held Buster for a time on my lap, his paws slowly pedaling, then took a cab to the airport, and flew.

Rental car from BWI down 97 to 50 past Annapolis to Woods Landing. When I parked, my mother was dressed up and ready to go.

Let's go to the Severn Inn, she said. You know the Severn?

Yep, I said, as it's where we always go.

She was dying to be out among people, young people, any people, *men*. When we got to the restaurant I helped her clump with her candy-bright cane across the deck to a table looking over the river to the Naval Academy, and the sun hung low and red, and we agreed it was grand to be out on the water on a warm summer eve, two single ladies on the town. When the wine came we toasted her birthday and talked about some birthdays past, and after a while I told her the rationales and ramifications of my decision to retire from love.

Well, well, she said. You know, darling, this might be how it *is* with our line of women. There's nothing my mother liked more than being alone in her house in Adelaide, tending her garden, making pavlova. And there's nothing I like more than being alone in *my* house, with the deck and tulip trees and paper. That might just be how our line is: contented, solitary women.

I nodded, and we gazed at the melting sun, the water tin-bright, not the green-blue of paradise, and I didn't have the heart to mention the difference between my mother and her mother, and me.

But oh well, it did feel grand to be out with her as in old days, and sitting with her cane hooked behind the chair she looked like herself. She glanced around gaily in her chartreuse top with her imbalanced seawater eyes, and she smiled widely at a pair of cadets and waved to a little girl in a puff of pink dress trotting up and down the deck, and even though we hadn't eaten, her wineglass was already empty. The waitress appeared and said, Another? and that mother of mine is always so fast that before I could say anything she nodded passionately and said, I should *think* so. Do you know I'm eighty today?

Well, happy birthday! sang the waitress, and the small girl by the rail spun to see.

The new glass came, was gulped down at once, too little of her crab cake was eaten and almost none of her green tomatoes, and I thought dammit, she takes lots of pills, but okay, it's her birthday, let her be jolly. Then as we were leaving, after I'd helped her clump down the ramp and across the asphalt to the car, as I was propping open the door with one hand and holding her elbow with the other, she began, slowly, to fall.

I have seen and seen this moment. It is slower every time.

She was clutching my wrist with one hand, her purse with the other, and one foot had veered into the passenger well, but the horizon must have tilted or her thin leg suddenly failed, because then her fingers were digging into my skin, she was falling slowly back, she had suddenly turned so heavy I could not hold her, I could not hold her, and she tilted backward and slid out of my hands and fell, her head hard on the asphalt.

Mom, I said, Mom!

She murmured something, and I was on my knees trying to lift her shoulders, her head, her hair slick with blood.

Help! We need help.

Then as people ran and called, as she lay on the ground and I pressed my scarf to her head to stop the blood, but it would not stop because of the Plavix, and I said, Mom, Mom, Mom, she began to make a noise. A deep grunting, something that could come from a bear or the ground. She muttered and grunted, her arms and legs stiffened like branches, and when she opened her eyes and stared at me, there was nothing I knew in that face.

In the ambulance they wouldn't let me in the back with her so I sat in the front, clasped her purse, and tried to follow the roads we took so I could find our way home. Route 50 to 97 to 695 and into Baltimore but then what? At the hospital—which hospital? Shock-Trauma something—they raced to wheel her in one door and shouted for me to go in another and find her inside. Find her inside. Find her inside. I ran through sliding doors, down halls, through more sliding doors, up steps, down more halls. When I found her she was in a sheeted place with people moaning on either side, blanket to her shoulders, face pointing above, pointing because her eyes and cheeks had suddenly sunk and she was nothing but nose.

I took her cold hand. She opened an eye and held my hand tight.

Something happened, she muttered.

Yes. But you'll be fine.

Mm, she said, and shut the eye.

I rubbed her knuckles. After a moment she squinted.

Am thinking, she said, of alphabet. Got to hyena.

(Her animal game.)

Hyena, I said. Okay: iguana.

A pale smile appeared. Iguana. Was that . . . in Ecuador? Did we live there?

Yes, we did. Your turn.

She shut her eyes, then said, What?

Next animal. Starting with J.

Oh. J. Jaguar.

Kangaroo.

She was silent again, her hand chill in mine.

Your turn, I said.

Where?

What?

Are we in hospital? she said.

I'm afraid we are.

In ... Maryland?

Yes!

Thought I lived there.

You do! Still your turn.

What?

Next animal.

Oh. Rather sleep a bit.

But right now we really don't want you to sleep.

She looked at me, and I stroked the hair from her brow, where skin is so shockingly thin.

And we moved on to L, and she said lynx, and I thought it might be good to change the game and asked how much *lynx* was worth, and she tried and gave up but I made her do it, count up the letters, and so it went for two hours, three, after we'd gone through animals we went through plants and then cities, her hands colder and drier, feet paddling quietly under the blanket, while near us a man screamed and another man tried to calm him, as we waited for someone to scan her brain, to tell us she was herself. When it was quiet but still wasn't morning, she looked up and whispered, Don't leave.

Of course not, I said. Where would I go?

• • •

The yolky next day, I walked through white halls and swinging doors and down stairs and through more doors until I found one to the world: morning sun, men laughing and smoking by a taxi stand. I called N.

Of course, she said. Don't worry about anything *here*. You take care of your mother, and I'll take care of little Buster, because that's how it ought to work in the world. Right? I'll send you pictures so you'll know he's fine.

At last it was confirmed: seizure but no stroke, no marks on her brain. We sat side by side and studied the images on the screen as the neurologist clicked through them, beautiful, grainy gray images shifting slightly at each click like paint-on-glass, islands and bayous and eddies moving behind the bone of her nose. How lovely, my mother murmured, and, looking at the swirls and pools, I wondered which held the traces of her dancing the cancan in Indonesia, striding down a Delaware beach, riding the Metro at dawn to teach at Federal Triangle and riding it home again at dusk, twirling over the brown-and-gold rug, spilling her wine or martini, licking the tongue of one of those men at the kitchen table, being hit by another and driving in rage over a Los Angeles freeway, all the traces of the husbands and men and other husbands and men, and tending her plants, willfully killing her plants, finding a dead hummingbird and keeping it in the freezer to look at now and then, all the traces somewhere in the beautiful myriad whorls and labyrinths of this brain we watched shift on the screen.

So there seems to be no damage, said the doctor. Just the previous problem with balance.

My mother looked bright. So I can go, she said. I can go home?

We'll see, he said. First let's see how well you get around on your own.

I thought, Could it *be*?

She got herself more or less attached to a walker, but couldn't fully rise and tumbled back on the bed. Second try she made two steps but then began sinking until she was caught.

Right, he said. Nope. We can't release you to live alone.

She stared at him a moment and then threw back her head.

I suppose the gods have spoken! she cried.

Are there options? he asked me. Resources? Assisted living possible—?

Rehab first, then Sunrise. Two weeks to get things in order.

Oh, she said, flinging up her hands. Just sell everything. I don't want anything. Only my books and birds.

Photo albums?

No, no, she said. Who cares about *them*. I don't want the past.

In the grocery store then, not in an aisle for pet goods or babies, but one for adults, I looked for pull-ups, small.

Back at rehab, helped her stand from the toilet, then coaxed up the pull-ups as she clutched my arms. I looked at her wobbling bare legs.

There you are, I said, making sure the pull-ups were snug on her hips, feeling Buster's skinny shanks.

When I'd cleaned her house, boxed up her books and clothes and her carved hoopoes, anhingas, and cockatoos, then filled out the forms for Sunrise and signed on with a realtor, I went to Bayridge rehab to say good-bye. She was curled like a shrimp in her bed, a thin arm over her eyes. The AC was too strong, sheer curtain blowing between her and a huge woman in the next bed snoring at a loud TV, a tattooed junkie rolling around in the hall. I shut the door, turned everything off, opened the window to summer air, sat on the bed, stroked her arm. And wondered where she was wandering in her mind, and whether the passages were getting more narrow, like veins.

She turned, opened an eye, and sighed.

Ah, well, she said. I suppose it's time.

Yep. Got a cat and a duck that need me.

And Ovid.

Sure.

We went over all the things that would be happening now, and after a while she put her hand on mine.

You know, she said, I don't think I meant what I told you. About how you should give up on all that, be alone.

Well, you know I never listen to you anyway, I said.

Because what will happen, she said, when you're like me, when this time comes, and you don't have someone like you?

Flying back to Miami that night, I stared at the thin line of light edging the coast from the blackness of ocean.

Then it was our turn to swing west and fly over the Venetians, and how beautiful they were, circles of light on the dark bay, small islands knee-deep in the sea.

Insula was island, for Ovid.

Later turned into *isola*.

Insulation, isolation.

Am wondering if they're really alike.

Walking down the long passages of Miami International, I couldn't stop staring at the gorgeous floor: terrazzo inset with tiny brass figures of plankton, sea fans, corals, algae, gastropods, urchins—tiny brass cells of life. Then the hallway reached a huge hub to other halls, so I looked up to find my way. Then down again to find a different floor. No tiny brass plankton inset in this terrazzo; instead, an enormous single pattern. A whorl of black and gray and white marble chips that spun and spun around a central eye: a hurricane of stone.

AND SHE'S RIGHT, my mother. N and K, too. Because I do remember moments, warm, voluptuous moments, what it could be like. One morning, when I was showered and warm and somehow feeling both porous and whole, in he came, into the room with its tall window of live oaks making the light green, the polished wood warm beneath my bare feet. The door clicked shut, and his sudden mouth on my neck felt river-fresh, my panties only just pulled on now slipped off by his fingers as I leaned back on the bed and sighed, my arms stretched over the cotton blanket, as what felt new and morning-clean slid inside to a place that was still blurred with sleep but waking so quickly, suddenly so full of quickness and light and pleasure, pleasure, until each of us was laughing in the other's laughing mouth. A morning like that, who wouldn't laugh with delight when it's wonderful and already done before you even knew you were longing?

Soft skin alive near your own, skin so close it isn't substance but pure human warmth. So close you can't imagine aloneness.

And I miss this. I miss it.

FOUR

FIRST DAY BACK at the Love Boat was the last day of the pool, and when I went down this morning, the hourglass was full of old swimmers, dismay. The lady with iron hair walked her grim circles in the shallow end; Fran's pink cap barged along the pool's rim, until she bumped into a carbuncled man leaning on the lip, his eyes shut and arms outstretched, old legs swaying in her path. I didn't swim, just lay on a lounge chair looking at words or up at the sky, and let the old swimmers have the pool.

After feeding the duck this evening, walked along the dock, past *Tango*, *All In!* and the little red ferry. Then up the spiral staircase, past the diving girl-tree, through the jungle. Flossy red bottle-brushes, alabaster beads dangling from a palm, yellow orchid blossoms on a tree whose name I've never learned. Planted near the rails to face the light-girl a last time before the pool was emptied and the jungle razed was the old man I've unkindly called the Mummy. His sculpted face, fine white hair combed neatly back, wheelchair fitted with tubes, blue-scrubbed attendant at either side, his eyes behind sunglasses, mouth ajar. One of the attendants rose when I passed, to dab the corners of his mouth, but the old man stared unseeing at the dancing light-girl as she threw her hair and swung her hips way across the bay.

Behind him, alone in the last hour of the hourglass pool, was N. In the evening light and the water's cool blue, her thin body seemed pale wax. She floated. Her eyes were shut, hair in wet tendrils, cheeks drawn, all long nose. She floated, still, suspended in blue. Then she gathered from her center, spread slim arms and legs, and began to swim. She swam parabolas and loops, ellipses and arcs, she swam a silent tale that seemed to tell who she was when still herself, which she would always and only be when she was in water.

Upstairs, I called my mother, Buster languorous on the sofa beside me, one paw draped over my leg.

You know, she said, I don't care how it looks, these old legs and arms and this ugly old wheelchair. It doesn't matter. Because *really* I'm still nineteen. Inside.

Nineteen somewhere deep inside, in the dark living pith at the core. Ovid's girls, the breathing trees.

Across the way, only one balcony of Costa Brava is lit, the corner of the seventeenth floor. Sitting there as in a niche of a shadowy church is the young woman with origami. Cross-legged, she works on pieces of colored paper, folding, gluing, cutting. Around her grows a nest of color.

First the contractors taped orange DANGER signs to the glass doors on the mezzanine and the top of the spiral steps. When everyone defied the signs, they added strips of DO NOT CROSS tape; finally they padlocked the doors and hung chains. They began draining the pool: sump pumps sucked water into big black rubber hoses that snaked over the balustrade down to the dock and spewed out to the bay. Then they buzz-sawed the jungle—palms, bottlebrushes, mahoganies, gumbo-limbos, screw pines crashing down. The smaller things they bulldozed, the philodendra, button trees, sweet olives, and others whose names I don't know, with flagrant yellow blossoms.

Let us take the small ones and put them in pots! cried people at a meeting. The lady upstairs was one.

Not cost-effective, said the contractor's spokesman. Don't worry. We'll plant new.

But that will take years!

And we are old.

It took three days to raze the jungle and drain the pool. No hourglass of clear blue, no tropical shadow, nothing but muddy concrete in raw sun. They left just one strip of the jungle standing, near the spiral steps, twenty-two stories below N and P.

SINCE THEN, IT'S rained. It rains every day.

No swimming, no walking. Just pacing inside the long vegetal halls.

Today the weather is deepening. The sky lowers, troubled, dense and gray, the air hot and tense. Tropical storm, everyone says. You can tell something's coming not just because of the sky but because men at Costa Brava are piling up lounge chairs and carting them inside. Up and down the building, plants and patio chairs are dragged in, hurricane shutters clattering shut.

But nothing's really happening yet, just that roiling sky, the water of the bay lead-dull and choppy, the few sailboats out there seesawing. No rain now. And after four pages of O I have got to get out of here and walk, hard and fast.

Of course I was out there when it hit, and when it did, it was wild. First a tingle in the air, a yellowish light as if from the ground, then a pull upward, a whoosh, and suddenly rain slashed down. Was on San Marino, three islands away, and the rain fell so hard, no point to my pink umbrella. Walked fast, then started to jog, and by the time I reached the next green verge, water bubbled up from the drains. By Di Lido it gushed down the gutters, and soon it sheeted over the street. By Rivo Alto it flowed up to my ankles, clothes dripping, water sliding into my eyes, my feet slipping out of the FitFlops, so took them off, to hell with glass. Tried really to run but the water rushed at my shins, and at the verge by the drawbridge, waves broke on the grass. The duck! She huddled in her sea grape, the shrub leaning, leaves tearing off and spinning into the wind. Nothing to do: I ran past. Waves rolled and crashed below the bridge, water spraying through the grate. Was over the bridge and over the verge and rounding the corner, struggling to move through flowing water, cars stalled everywhere, people in them looking stunned or climbing out, staggering through surf like me.

Up ahead on the ramp to the front entry was Virgil, tie in the wind, trying to get a white-coiffed lady inside.

Faster to come in through the garage, where water spewed from the drain holes, gushed through the rebar skeleton of the pool, rivered over the concrete floor. Got in the elevator and rose to my floor, and when I'd run squelching down the hall, opened my door in time to see the green table skidding over the porch— so wrenched the sliding doors open to the roaring wild and pulled in the table and chair that had already slammed against the wall. Got the glass doors shut and locked, water on the cork as far as the couch, and could see almost nothing beyond the balustrade, only gray blur, streaming, leaves and trash whipping by. And so loud, a roaring and shrieking, glass vibrating violently. I found Buster, held him tight, went into the closet, shut the door.

We sat there, curved together in the dark. Buster shivered, feeling the thunder and howling wind even if he couldn't hear them. I stroked his small head and the slender gully between his shoulders and held him nestled in my lap, his once clear eyes staring blind at the dark, his diaper loose, hind legs trembling. We rocked in the dark as the wind screamed and rain roared, his pin-claws kneading my shoulder, whiskers at my cheek.

I will always love you, no matter what, my husband whispered one night near the end, before we finally gave up.

• • •

And maybe that's enough. To have had some love some time. Even if it worked only awhile. It's enough to have had some once and now to live with just pieces of it, and it's all right if you spend what you still have on an old cat or duck, a few friends, your mother. Not everyone is paired on the ark.

WHEN I GOT up this morning and went into the study, I knew even before opening the door. A stillness.

Buster lay on the cork, thin black paws crossed. I stroked his head; the silky fur was cool. Sank my hands and face in his soft belly. Knelt there awhile.

After a time, called N.

Oh, no, I'm sorry, she said. I'm so sorry. She sounded like she was about to cry, too, large gray eyes going liquid.

At least I didn't do it, I said. Should I have?

No, she said, her voice firm. He was home. With you. No.

She told me to come up and have a drink.

When you feel like it, she said. How about six? I'm not feeling so hot myself, to tell the truth, but a drink would be nice.

Laid Buster in his nest. Decided he could stay there today.

Seemed best only to read, today. Look at the water, the sky.

WHEN I WENT up to N's place, she looked like I'd caught her at something, her eyes wild above that stalk of neck.

No, it's okay, she said. Come on, let's have some wine. Or maybe a martini. I could use a martini. But I'll get you wine.

We sat on the balcony, looking down at the ruined jungle, cratered pool, islands, and distant city, talking about the last days of pets, and something faltered in her voice.

No no, she said, I'm sorry. It's the same stupid thing, it's just this *pain* I can't get rid of, even after the last procedure, I didn't even tell you about it, I'm a big fool to have done it, and this isn't me, I wish you didn't know me like this, really I used to be a lot of fun— and her eyes were filling, her flossy head quavering on that neck, but just then there was a noise from inside the apartment.

Oh. That's P, she said. He likes to let me spend myself for a time on people, and when I get to a certain point, he'll come out and change the subject. Right, P? There you are.

P stepped out onto the porch with a bottle and glass. He looked fixedly at N, then turned to me. It seemed like a good time to join you, he said.

N turned away. I try not to talk about it. I hate talking about it, but then.

I'm sorry, I said. I wish—

She raised a thin yellow hand.

I'm sorry, P said, about your cat.

Realized I'd never thanked him for the hammerhead, so did.

What's this? He gave you a *shark*?

A photo, P said. She didn't believe they were down there. There's probably one right now.

We all looked over the balcony rail, toward the bay, its silver-black gleams.

Well, of course she should believe you, N said. Just like you have to believe me. Even though it's *invisible*. Sometimes we have to take people at their word.

I do believe you, N, he said. You know that.

I know, she said, I know. I'm sorry. These *drugs*. She shook her head hard. Although honestly I don't know how you can, she said. When you can't see any signs of it—and that *doctor*, what he insists—how you can believe . . .

He put his hand on her arm. She took a breath, a sip, and we all looked again at the bay.

From up there the river in the water was clear, a different color, the sea current that rushes through the Government Cut. I thought of that drowning man and told them.

Right there, I said. In the current.

Christ, P said. Lucky you saw him and called.

But I didn't. I didn't have my phone. I just—

That man, said N, a few weeks ago? Is that what you're talking about? I only just realized what you were talking about.

You saw him?

Sure. I'm sitting out here all the time.

What did you do?

Well, actually I heard him before I saw him.

Why didn't you tell me? said P.

What's to tell?

What's to tell? That a man's drowning and needs help!

But what did you do? I said.

What do you think?

You called?

Of course.

You're the one who called?

Sure, she said.

P looked at her. You saved him, he said.

So I picked up the phone, N said. What's the big deal? You dial three little numbers! You don't let somebody *drown*.

The clouds smoldered, edges flaming, long rays of light.

No, said P. That's true.

As if I need to tell you two that, said N. You, who've taken care of Buster forever, to say nothing of that *duck*. And this man who takes such care of me. This good good good *good* man— Here, she said, I'll even give you my olive.

Only because you hate the olive!

She was laughing and reaching to him when suddenly there came that look in her eyes. He took her hand, held it locked.

After a moment she said, Well, will you just look at that sky. But wait a minute. Wait a minute. I just remembered. P, tell her about what happened during the storm the other day.

That was something.

Tell her.

It was ... what, last Monday?

Just as the storm was coming, said N.

And I thought I had at least an hour—

See how wrong you were? I told you, I could see, it was moving fast—

So anyway, he said, I was down in the boat—

He said he *had* to tie something, said N.

In the what? I said.

The boat, said P.

I never mentioned it? said N.

Right down there, said P.

Here?

Down to the left.

The green one?

No. Beside it.

Red?

Enough already, said N. Tell her.

I need another drink first. Anyone?

Nodded.

P refilled our glasses and, as the sky behind him slowly darkened over the ruined jungle and the bay where a hammerhead might be swimming, and the island where a girl might be walking into the HAREM house, and the next island where a man might be stepping out of the ground, and the water between islands where a man might be standing and rowing into the dusk, and as I tried to erase my secret pictures of the man in black who was P, he told what happened in the storm.

He'd been in the boat as it rolled in, trying to do something to make the boat safe, which he explained in detail but I quit following. The boat had been rocking hard, lurching side to side so that he could barely stand, when suddenly there was a shattering crack: electricity branched from the sky, struck his antenna, and threw him back, a tree of light as the bolt raced down the rod and into the water, shot out in lines to the depths.

When he was finished telling, it had fallen dark. No twilight in Miami. Boats bobbed, their bouncing lights and the lights' liquid ghosts. The city skyline was lit red, white, and green. The huge bright girl danced alone in the air with her swinging hair and hips and boots. P looked at his hands, cradled in his lap.

Christ, I said.

I still can't believe it, said N.

Me neither.

That you didn't get the bolt itself.

No.

We were silent, sipping our drinks.

But I'll get the boat fixed, said P. And when it's fixed, we'll take you out. That be fun?

Yes, I said. Yes. Please.

And I saw N smile in the dark.

On the way to my apartment, I stopped at the landing outside and looked down to the glittering black bay, to where the palm frond had become a shark, and pictured the hammerhead, swaying its scalloped head as it searched the lightless deep.

Back in my apartment, with no Buster, just a little black form waiting in his nest, I slid open the glass doors and went out to the balcony. Costa Brava, where no one seemed to be home, hurricane shutters blanking most of the windows, and beyond it, the thin strip of lit city, and beyond that, beyond the invisible beach, the black sea beneath the dark sky.

Blue glow at my hand.

I wish I knew how to help her. I don't. Don't answer, please—there's nothing to say. I just have to say it sometimes.

Far out at sea, heat lightning. A silent splinter of light, a lingering flare.

Drove over to the Beach, north up Collins to the Forties. Got out, walked to where the sand is almost white, and filled a bag. At home, poured the sand into a small box and carefully placed Buster there as if he were lounging on the beach. He would never have lounged on the beach—the one time I took him there, thinking he'd gambol after pipers or crabs, he clung near my feet like a tight plush shadow in all that bleached space. But now he looked peaceful, paws crossed, long white whiskers and eyebrows alert. I stroked his long ears and tender cheeks, then fastened the lid. Put a ribbon around the box and held the box close as I rode down to the mezzanine, the flamingo mirrors and slow stirring fans, out through the last strip of jungle, around the spiral staircase, to the far corner of the dock. Knelt, rested the box on the milky green water, whistled a little from *Last Tango*, let go. The box tilted, bubbled, sank.

My apartment's so still now. No howls, no puddles or diapers, no purr. Walked through it barefoot feeling for whiskers or eyebrows left on the cork. Found five and glued them into my Oxford edition of O.

Now there's nothing but O. Just sink into his words, his golden crossed lines, their patterns and sounds, and through them to his figures, a girl writing a bold note to her brother, a boy touching a pool's delicate skin. All those girls and boys two thousand years old: but still here with me, still alive, still changing. Each phrase sinks into my eyes and blood and after a time emerges new, in another language, an altered tale, but these words feel, they really do feel, like him, his voice, my O.

Came out to the balcony and looked down at the glittering world for a while, then up at the deepening blue. No boys are falling into the sea, only star-planes coming and coming. Went inside for dinner, a drink. Now light-strung cruise ships pass through the Government Cut and slip into liquid night.

And maybe, you know, my O is enough. Maybe it's not bad to love so much what another mind made.

A kind of marriage, maybe.

HAVE BARELY SEEN N and P since that night. No pool deck to find them on anyway, but they seem even further removed than that, locked in something alone. I did run into her in the elevator and was startled and said, How *are* you? But her pink-rimmed eyes turned to tears, she opened her mouth but shook her head and walked out as soon as she could.

From my balcony I sometimes see her and P in the park, though, walking slowly along the path. She's so frail he holds her elbow.

It's hard not to look away. Yet an afterimage burns: P, strong and alive, walking with a skeleton. An ugly thing to think, but I can't help it, and you can tell other people see this, too.

Went upstairs last week with a book I'd promised her, but as I was about to knock there came from inside a sound—a keening. I hesitated, set the book against the door, walked back down the hall. Before I'd turned the corner, their door opened with a flow of light, and P stepped out. He didn't see me. He stood in the hall, door shut behind him, pressing his hands to his eyes.

Have left a new book every few days since then. I send messages, too, but she doesn't write back, won't answer the phone.

But P was in the garage today, that underworld now ripped with light where the pool's frame has been stripped of concrete.

N doesn't mean to be rude, he said. She just can't—she can't be with people these days. If she opens her mouth there's only one thing she can say.

And—

He shook his head and turned to go, but stopped.

Did you know I met her in college? he said. Yep. She was sitting on the green with a notebook, I looked over, she looked up, that was it.

He laughed a little, pushed the button for the grate to rise, ducked under it to the blaze.

Y OU'VE SEEN TREES that twine together. Maybe you know this story. It's almost the last I'll tell. Those entwined trees, often two dogwoods, one with coral flowers, the other ivory: do their trunks actually meld? Can they? Can skin become porous? This story's not about young people—we've had enough of them. Two old people, a long time wed. So used to each other, even their movements have grown the same, their hair, their hands, their gaits. Although sometimes you see old couples that are fantastically unlike: a rail of a man with a woman so bent she sees only her feet; he is her periscope as they inch on. Often saw this couple from my window in Germany. Anyway, this other pair, when they look at each other, can no longer remember the difference between them, and what they'd felt when they first saw each other—maybe on a green, one sitting reading, the other balancing on a rope tied between trees before he saw her and fell—what they felt that first moment, they do still. With more complexity now, layers of sediment and time, but pretty much the same. So. It is now many years after that first sighting. They have grown old, and it is almost time. She is sick. Neither can bear it. One night, each of them, alone, not wanting to worry the other, looks up at the stars and whispers the same hope.

Somewhere in the distance, a glow.

In the morning, the wife is much weaker. She looks at her husband, he looks at her, in all eyes is panic, their fingers interlace—but then somehow they lace even more, these fingers strangely longer than usual, longer and somehow not feeling the same, but twisting and twining about one another! The husband and wife look on, amazed, as those fingers now grow velvety green and sprout small glossy leaves, their hands and wrists start turning vine—so do their arms and breasts, bellies and chest, their two bottoms, four legs, and then their faces can only look at each other and say Oh! and smile through tears of sap before they too are green and gone in stem and leaf, growing and twining still closer, closer, and there will be no end.

J UST NOW, out at sea, a flare of lightning. Haze around a jag of light, and in it I see N. In the next one, I see P.

A FINAL TRY to capture the duck. Did not go prepared. Just saw her as I approached the verge and couldn't stand it, had to catch her, grab her, take her somewhere else.

Dusk, the grassy verge, the blades moist and tickling, my Fit-Flops making the thwack at which she turns her head. She waddled toward me as I came near, my eyes on one of her pink-rimmed black eyes, Grape-Nuts in a baggie in hand. I did not go to our usual meeting point but stopped in the middle of the grass, crouched, strewed kernels, then moved backward, drawing a path of grains that would Hansel-and-Gretel her to me. She gobbled from the first pile, followed the trail five or six inches—but then sensed something and lifted her head. Only four paces from my knees. I should have waited until she came. I should have just been patient.

But couldn't stand it. I tightened, then sprang—

And the duck: she flapped and suddenly wobbled up into the air. She beat her wings hard and wobbled and rose, careened right at me so I had to crouch, then flew above me, rose higher, higher, began to soar, swerved from the verge, and wheeled over the bay.

I sat on the grass and cried.

When I got home, two police cars were again parked on the ramp, blue lights spinning soundless. I went around back to walk along the dock and look as always into the water. When I spiraled up the steps to the last strip of paradise jungle, three policemen stood by the windows near the gym, yellow tape on the ground.

TWO PEOPLE SLOWLY cycling in our gym on the mezzanine, two people staring west through the glass as they pedaled, saw N when she fell.

Although she didn't fall. You don't fall off a balcony on the twenty-second floor. You get up from your chair, push it to the railing, climb up, maybe balance on the edge a minute, look over, look back, look away. Then you decide it's time.

The two saw a crash in the green.

The police had to take a picture and show it to people in apartments all the way up to the twenty-second floor before they found someone who knew N. It was the woman above me, the one with the garden, who finally said who she was.

Low plants that are pale green and cream and look like sea grass: that's where she landed. Between a fan palm and a ponytail tree. She seems to have aimed for them. Walking around all those days in her bikini, large wet footprints on the path, deciding what to do.

Ice cubes, she was dropping.

And P is not here. He is in Canada. But was on his way home when he got the call. It seems that she planned it this way.

• • •

Virgil told me all this as I walked back and forth and back and forth on the dock.

Maybe it felt like swimming?

If you retire from love, N once told me, then you retire from *life*.
    N is the one who said this.

IT'S ALMOST eleven. The police cars are still parked on the ramp, but their blue lights no longer spin. The police themselves wait upstairs in the apartment for P, wait until one of the planes that fly in is his.

I wait, too.

The planes appear, one star swelling after another, and it's a strange emergence each time a new star grows out of that dark. But they do, they keep emerging from that darkness, growing brighter until finally swerving west. P is on one of these, maybe the one turning now, maybe up there now looking down at the blackness of sea, lights frilling the shore. And if he is on that one, he sees the bright strip of beach, the high red lights showing pilots the topography of roofs. He can see our islands spangled upon black.

One star has just made the turn and transformed from pure light to jet. I will sit here and wait until his plane has flown over and landed ten miles west, until he's picked up the bag of clothes recently folded for him by N, stepped into a cab, and sped over the causeway, back to this island where his wife is not. At last a cab will pull up the ramp slowly, in consideration for the man inside.

This might be him, this cab now. I think it's him. The driver's stepped out, walked around to the trunk, pulled out a bag, set it down.

In the fountain by the entryway, water jets, tumbles, and falls— its sound.

When it is P, everything will begin. He will come inside, ride the elevator up to his floor, and walk the long hall to his doorway. The police will take him out to the balcony and show him where N stood, where she pulled a chair to the rail. They will stand on each side of P as he takes this in with his eyes. But his eyes will find, in the potted palm on the balcony, a single toothpicked olive, and he won't be able to help it, he'll see her sipping a last martini before dumping the olive she never liked, before she does what she does at 6:17, and he won't be able to help it: he'll laugh. The police will escort him in to the kitchen table, where she placed her letter, and maybe then or maybe later he will read it: the words are words he knows. Yet she will tell him a few new things. How she'd been ready to do this three months before but decided to wait a bit: she wanted to leave things in order. He'll see how carefully she planned, how she deliberated her method. One that's unusual for a woman but likely to succeed. She'll tell him things he knows but needs to see again, and others he does not need to see again, does not wish ever to see again, wishes he could scrub from the earth. She'll even tell him a few things she'd had in mind these past months, matters she'd hoped to set in motion, in leaving him alone. She did not want him to be alone. Or me.

The cab door opened. P stepped out. The door shut, and the cab pulled away, curved down the ramp, around the oval park, was gone. But P still stood on the curb. For a moment, as long as he didn't move, he might stand outside time. The only thing moving were the cords and sprays of water as the fountain jetted up in the light, weakened, tumbled, splashed a chlorine bloom.

Far to the right in the sky, a light appeared. From Brazil, maybe, or Peru.

P bent for his bag. As he rose he lifted his face and seemed suddenly to see our huge building. He stood staring up at the height.

I was in the lobby by then, with Virgil. We both looked away; we had to.

Just the sound of the rising, falling, splashing water. Everything else was still.

Then P was stepping onto the curb, and we were stepping out, the revolving door turning, Virgil reaching to touch his arm, starting to say something, and what could he say, and I was behind, the same—

But there came a sudden sharp whistle from across the way, from Costa Brava. We all stopped and looked.

The origami woman stood on her balcony on the seventeenth floor, holding a nest of colored paper. It looked like a fabulous cape, a dancer's skirts. She went to the balustrade and called down a word to someone waiting. It took her a moment to gather herself, and then, in a sweep, she flung the paper over the balustrade rail. It fell like smoke, billowing and slow, a chain of colors, a rope of sky and coral and lime, colors that spooled, cascaded.

We watched as it swung and slowly stilled in the night. Then she waved to her friend below, and he waved smiling back up to her, camera in his hand.

Virgil took P's arm, I took his bag, and we walked through the revolving door.

OVID, STILL here?

I like to think I see your eyes. I like to think I hear you. I do feel your sentences swimming inside, your figures pacing their wilds of woods, and air, and letters, and time.

The idea that your words could ever be dead, past not always present.

Try telling that to the sand, the sea.

Acknowledgments

Brief passages from writers and lyricists other than Ovid appear, sometimes paraphrased, in these pages: Yeats's "Sailing to Byzantium," channeled through William Gass's "In the Heart of the Heart of the Country"; the opening lines of Dante's *Inferno* (my translation); Coleridge's "Rime of the Ancient Mariner"; the Clash's "Should I Stay or Should I Go?"; Kate Bush's "Wuthering Heights"; Chrissie Hynde's "Talk of the Town" and "Up the Neck"; Marianne Faithfull's "Why'd Ya Do It?"; James Brown's "Get Up (I Feel Like Being a) Sex Machine"; David Bowie's "Ashes to Ashes"; John Mayer's "Your Body Is a Wonderland"; and David Markson's *Wittgenstein's Mistress*.

For their care in helping me bring this to printed page, my great thanks to Lauren Groff, David Shields, Karen McBryde, Andrea Barrett, Emily Forland, and Pat Strachan, with her wonderful team at Catapult.

About the Author

Jane Alison is the author of a memoir, *The Sisters Antipodes*, and three novels—*The Love-Artist*, *The Marriage of the Sea*, and *Natives and Exotics*—and is also the translator of Ovid's stories of sexual transformation, *Change Me*. She is professor and director of creative writing at the University of Virginia and lives in Charlottesville. www.janealison.com